Trials

THANE KELLER

ISBN: 0-9969224-4-X
ISBN-13: 978-0-9969224-4-9

DEDICATION

To my wife Sarah - words could never describe how much you mean to me - I am nothing without you.

PROLOGUE

"Make no mistake," the speaker said resolutely, "with this technology and your continued investment, we could terraform an entire planet!" The audience erupted in applause, and the attractive female scientist smiled widely behind her podium. After years of research on volcano fields and at the bottom of the ocean, she was finally getting her big break. Jillian looked over to three older gentlemen in light gray three button suits seated to her right. These were the corporate drones funding her research and Jillian was convinced that not one of them ever once had an original thought. They clapped and smiled. One gave her an approving nod, and she turned back to the crowd of eager donors.

"Now that I've explained my research behind the concept, I want to show you the progress we have already made in this exciting new field and the direction we are going." Jillian stepped to the side and gripped a thin silver remote in her palm. Clearing her throat, she looked to the back of the room and asked the audiovisual crew to dim the lights. Instantly, the auditorium was dark, and the image of a plant appeared on the screen. The plant was tall, with a sturdy green stock and large green leaves that stretched upward and then bowed to the ground under its own weight. Judging from the slide, the plant was approximately five feet tall, but more peculiar than that, the picture captured a faint green glow emitting from the leaves themselves.

"This is a kelp and corn hybrid infused with the genetic makeup of bacteria that lives on the ocean floor. Rather than require water, it feeds almost entirely on sulfur and still generates oxygen, not from photosynthesis, but from a direct reaction to carbon dioxide. You may notice the green glow on the slide. This isn't bad camera work," Jillian said with a smile, to chuckles in the audience, "the green glow is actually a reaction from bacteria that are living on the leaf in a symbiotic manner. These bacteria are actually generating luminescence as a result of a chemical reaction. But more importantly, the light they emit actually contains enough energy to provide a photosynthetic process for the remaining plants, and that is what we will address here. In other words", Jillian paused dramatically, "we've created a much weaker version of the sun!"

Flipping the slide, Jillian revealed a photo of red and green algae. "This algae feeds on iron as a result of genetic modification. Again, the byproduct is oxygen. You'll notice that while this algae doesn't emit a green light, it is happy to absorb the light which enables its own photosynthesis to take place. In this sense, the algae and the plants have a symbiotic relationship and contribute holistically to their environment. I hope you can see how we've really built a self-sustaining ecosystem for the harshest of places!"

After flipping through several other slides and explaining her various genetic hybrids, Jillian reached the final slide, a small earthworm. Placing her clicker down on the table, Jillian motioned for the lights to be turned back on. "I am going to reiterate an important point so that all of you can understand what we've created in these previous slides before we discuss our final breakthrough. All of these plants are designed to work symbiotically with each other so that they can literally create an environment that they can thrive in. The best part about this environment isn't just that it's capable of sustaining unique plant life; it is also capable of sustaining animal life. With that being said, the last of these is this genetically modified earth worm. In our preliminary tests, it has demonstrated itself to be a very resilient creature, capable of methodically transforming, fertilizing, and aerating the ground under the plants. As I said, it is a complete ecosystem." Jillian paused, adjusted her glasses, and read her final pitch. "With your continued support, we will complete this research and make even the least habitable places on earth livable again!"

The crowd gave generous applause, and Jillian stepped away from the podium and towards the three men seated behind her. They stood, shook her hand, and ushered her off the stage before any questions could be asked. "Did I do a good enough job selling it?" she asked, once away from the lights, cameras, and reporters.

"I see the heavens in your future," the gentleman replied.

CHAPTER 1

When the ground shook, it started off as a slow rumble, simply vibrating the metal springs on his twin-sized bed causing them to rattle back and forth against its steel frame. Ordinarily, he wouldn't have responded. The ground here had tremors frequently, and other than a little dust from the ceiling of their cavern home, there wasn't much excitement to be had.

He didn't get out much. At least, he didn't used to, but he thought back to his years in captivity frequently, and sometimes he even thought beyond that. The earthquake was the single point in time that changed his life for good. Before the earthquake, he wasn't just a nobody; he was worse than a nobody. He was a killer. A killer that was lost and forgotten in the depths of the most mind-numbing prison. But the earthquake. The earthquake changed all of that.

As he sat on his bed that day, he replayed the pivotal moment that led him down a path that would forever torment him; not because of the action he took, but because he feared he would never be able to feel that free again. For years, he was a prisoner in his own mind unable to act out the impulses that made him feel so free. He remembered watching the boy ride his bike back from school. Every day the boy passed his house. Every day he watched him. Finally, after much torment, he stepped outside.

He remembered the boy's shock at first, the fear that drenched his face. The surprise that a human being could be so cold. More importantly, he remembered how free he had felt afterward, how relieved he was that he could finally reveal himself to the world as he truly was. But then it ended, and all that was left was a memory. Until the earthquake.

Now, he was a king. Sitting high above his subjects, he ruled with sovereign power. An eye for an eye, a tooth for a tooth, and all people would give tribute to him. Minions and pawns scurried about around him, grateful that he had allowed them to live after that fateful day. The day that the gods had declared long ago was his for the taking. One cleaned, the other cooked. Others stood guard. He had sought this recognition for years and never found it. But he was an opportunist. And when opportunity struck, he seized power.

He wasn't large or tall, but he was smart. And he was vicious. All those years imprisoned in his own mind gave him time to think. That is what separated him from the others. He murdered because it was who he was, not because of his circumstances, but because of who he was at his very core. While others concerned themselves with revenge, or getting back at the guards, he went straight for the resources; the one thing that had to be controlled to force everyone else into subjection under his feet.

Then, all that was needed was to make an example of someone. To show the rest how absolutely brutal he could be. He didn't like to get his hands dirty when it came to politics, but that first one had to happen. Soon, others joined him. He consolidated resources and had something to offer. Food, shelter, and protection. All in exchange for unwavering loyalty. Eventually, all the people submitted to his rule.

Here, in this dark, chaos-filled place, he brought order. He brought meaning. He brought purpose. They called him Malek. King. And that's what he was to them. He was *their* King.

CHAPTER 2

The car was half submerged in the murky canal water. Soldiers on one side; frantic citizens on the other. A crowd gathered around the hasty rescue effort in the center. He could still see her in his mind. Not her face, but her back. Her hair gently dangled in the water as men pulled her out by her feet. The car had been submerged for almost 6 hours. Rescuers cheered as they finally pulled her out; she couldn't have been older than six or seven. They laid her down next to her mother. It was just another day in Iraq.

Jonah lay there sweating. He couldn't sleep. His mind jumped from Iraq to Afghanistan to the Sudan to eastern Russia. His thoughts weren't filled with guilt, or shame, or fear but a deeper form of questioning. One he could never put his finger on. He saw the girl again. Hair dipping into the water as she was lifted out. He always went back to the girl. Sometimes he imagined her frantically trying to escape the car. At the moment the water filled her lungs she was at peace, and he imagined that death for her was a better alternative to the life she might be forced to live. Eventually Jonah stopped trying to figure the events out and simply remembered them for what they were - crazy.

The cold damp cell where Jonah found himself could not be compared to the torment that had trapped his thoughts for years. But this was more than a cell and more complex than a standard prison. Jonah was locked away from the light of day and stowed deep underground where he couldn't hope to hear the laughter of his children or feel the touch of his wife ever again. He remained tormented in his mind, not only for the things he had done and saw, but also for things he could never do again.

His current circumstances made it laughable to think of even one blessing of God. And yet, in the cool dampness of night, with only the slightest whimper of other inmates to distract his thoughts, Jonah could easily find them. More often than not, those blessings existed in the form of memories - his three children and a wife that loved him deeply, remaining loyal in these dire circumstances. He also found them in his prison in the present. Jonah sensed them when the sounds of other inmates reminded him he wasn't alone, at the kindness of a guard giving him an extra portion of food, and every once in a while at the faintest ray of light that managed to penetrate a sewage vent at the end of their concrete hallway.

At Jonah's weakest, he cried bitterly. He had done so many times here while he counted the days of a trial that appeared to never be coming. He felt the absolute inadequacy to defend himself against a power that invented guilt and innocence rather than adhering to an absolute definition of righteousness. Tonight, however, his mind had no time to succumb to the self-imposed pity that he and countless others endured while at the mercy of the state. No, tonight he could only think of her. That young girl strung upside down by her feet as she was pulled from the concrete canal. Frail and lifeless, she was the mere shell of a body that was altogether empty of the soul that had once made her human. Sometimes he thought he might shed just one of his tears for her. But he couldn't. He didn't know her and had arrived too late to blame himself. She was just an image. A picture forever engrained in his mind. The first among hundreds he would see. But she was the first, and she was the only one entirely undeserving of the fate that gripped her.

Sometimes when images of the girl appeared in his mind, he would try to think of his family instead. He remembered the times he and his wife would spend on the playground watching their children laugh and giggle. He would fantasize about taking his children sledding, teaching them to hunt and fish, and watching them grow; all the while marveling with his beautiful wife at how large they'd gotten. Jonah imagined, with guilt, the missed opportunities too. How many years had he thrown away to his work and his job? How many months had he thrown away to this cell, imprisoned by the very people he had spent so many years protecting? Despite his attempts,

Jonah's mind always came back to the girl. That girl who so many years ago engrained herself into his mind for eternity. Eventually, on that cold, hard mattress in his damp, dark room, sleep overtook him; another blessing he took for granted all too often.

CHAPTER 3

"Clark, you're looking at it all wrong!" The sharply dressed Unicore executive argued over a cup of steaming coffee. His hair was as dark as the moonless night that hovered outside the windows of the coffee house. Jacob wore a black suit, a white neatly pressed shirt, and a red tie. The tie had a gold clasp that held it tidily against his shirt. Along the center of the clasp were four red triangles that formed the Unicore logo that so often graced their products.

Across the table sat Clark; a scruffy haired graphic designer with a three-day shadow and a cheap, tieless suit. Clark leaned across the table, over his caramel latte, and attempted to peaceably engage Jacob; clarifying what he meant.

Jacob wasn't interested. "You need to change your perspective.

We're offering opportunity. This is a chance to gain new skills and hone old ones. This is a privilege – to be one of the first men on the frontier of civilization."

Clark nodded and tried to follow along but was already distracted by the smell of fresh coffee beans and the promise of caffeine and sugar. He leaned back in his chair, enchanted by the ambiance of the diner, the smells of the coffee, and the dark cold night they were escaping. Jacob was reiterating a point he had already made but was now pressing the table forcefully with his index finger to exaggerate his emphasis.

"This is an opportunity for people that don't get opportunities. This is something that they can be proud of. Something future generations will be taught in schools. These are people that are on the frontier of human exploration. These people are heroes Clark, they're heroes. That's the point you need to drive home." Jacob hesitated and then continued. "Listen. We brought you in to give us a fresh look. Don't let us down." He paused a moment longer while Clark sat in silence and then made one final calculated statement. "Earth might not be around much longer, Clark."

Without waiting for a response, the advertising executive threw a ten dollar bill on the table, climbed out of the bench seat, and disappeared through the wooden door. Clark remained seated, milking the rest of his caramel latte as he pondered the challenge ahead of him and the cryptic warning that Jacob had left him with. *How do you convince someone to leave everything they know and take a one way trip to Mars?*

Artists drew creativity in different ways, and as for Clark, his was stimulated by people watching. Clark had long suspected that he could discern the motives and personality of a person simply by watching their actions and expressions when they thought no one was watching, and, in his line of work, he desperately needed to figure out what made people tick.

Looking around the espresso-colored coffee house, inhaling the fumes of various coffees, creamers, and pastries, Clark found himself fixated on a poster for a political rally. He didn't watch the news much, but he read enough to know what was happening to his country; and it wasn't good. In fact, minus an all-out succession, the lines had been essentially drawn in the sand between what some people were calling the red states and the blue states. The red states jumped on this division first and seized on the opportunity to rename themselves. They began to refer to the states in their coalition as 'Free States'. The Blue States, recognizing their disadvantage adopted a similar title – 'States of Opportunity.' This was a battle for hearts and minds, and despite his distance from the political scene, it was not lost on Clark that this was a war of public opinion. Those names reflected a leader's attempt at controlling thoughts, which was exactly why he appreciated it so much. In fact, the rhetoric was so strong that a red state senator was attacked by an angry mob outside of the capitol building in DC. According to some media outlets, the police did nothing and some even incited the mob to greater violence.

If Clark didn't watch the news much, he did even less considering of political issues, and, quite frankly, he wasn't sure he cared what each sides' grievances were. Art was Clark's escape from the world, and so long as he had a steady supply of customers and didn't live on the street, he was content to just not know. Regardless of which side ended up winning, losing, or separating, Clark wasn't sure much would change for him.

Two teenage girls climbed out of a booth to his right and giggled their way to the bathroom. Left behind were two shaggy-haired young men. As engaged as they were when the two girls were with them, they quickly sunk into the booth and pulled out phones. Entirely uninterested in talking to each other, they waited in silence for their dates to return. These were the people he loved to watch because, through his work, these were the people he would try so hard to convince.

CHAPTER 4

Moonlight reflected dimly off a picture that Evie had now been staring at thoughtfully for at least half an hour. She had stared at that photo hundreds of times for countless hours, but tonight, perhaps by the pale light of the moon, Evie noticed something she hadn't seen before. It was a picture of their wedding day, a photo of them with their parents. Everyone was staring at the camera except for Jonah. It looked like he was staring at the camera, but upon closer inspection in this particular light, it was clear he wasn't. His eyes weren't watching the camera at all. He was watching her. *How many times had she looked at this very picture and not noticed?* All of a sudden the joy of their wedding and the years they spent together came rushing back. Even if just for a moment, it was enough to make everything they had suffered together worth it. She refused to accept his guilt, and staring at this photo of so many years ago strengthened her resolve. She *would* see him again.

It would be another sleepless night full of uncertainty, sorrow, and fear. The knocks on their door six months ago initiated by two officers of the state had forever turned her world upside down. The slamming of the iron knocker resonated in her mind until she could no longer take it. Some nights were better than others. Tonight was not one of those nights. While the children slept, Evie snuck out of bed and went downstairs to turn on the TV.

Expecting typical late night programming, Evie was grateful to find an interesting documentary on the Mars colonization effort. Jillian Jaspers' determined and chunky little face was plastered on posters in every mall across America. She was the face of the Mars exploration and had inspired state and federal lotteries of willing (and desperate) families to get off Earth and travel to Mars.

In just ten short years, Jillian and her crew of early explorers had built a massive colony with the purpose of pursuing unique scientific research, all backed by companies exporting rare Earth minerals that were found in droves on the Red Planet. Gold, platinum, lithium, and copper were in abundance and instigated a colonization effort similar to the gold rush in California in the 1800s. The invention of quantum propulsion engines made the trip millions of dollars cheaper and thirty days shorter from the previous average of two hundred and ten days.

The documentary showed a lavish paradise of interconnected structures built under the Martian soil. Massive buildings were lined with the most expensive metals and decorated with the finest materials that could be mined. Hotels with vacation packages erupted overnight and commercials tugged at wealthy families who could afford the trip.

Like any colony, it wasn't without its troubles. Merely a few years after colonization, a contingent of marines was dispatched to the planet to restore order after a dispute broke out between two mining companies. They established a prison system, and under a United Nations mandate, imposed martial law. The United States government decided to capitalize on the establishment, of course, and saw it as a perfect chance to drain out the worst criminals in the U.S. Other countries followed suit, and not before long, Earth's worst convicts were sent to the first extraterrestrial penal colony. Although the documentary didn't say it, to Evie, Mars became the perfect juxtaposition: families seeking a permanent future and the pursuit of riches on the Red Planet occupied one side; while the world's worst convicts with no future occupied the world's harshest prison on the other.

Evie couldn't imagine leaving Earth willingly and permanently; in fact, it seemed like a death sentence regardless of which side you found yourself. Even with the early explorers of America, Evie found it hard to picture leaving a place as comfortable as this to get her name in the history books. Even if her town wasn't quaint and comfortable, it was still her town; and more importantly, it had oxygen and water – something that she determined was as good a reason as any to never go to another planet. As the documentary ended, Evie found the soft glow of the TV relaxing. Finally, sleep won; but it never lasted long.

****

The pitter patter of tiny feet down the hallway ripped Evie out of her late night rest and pulled her back to the present. Evie stared down at the skillet of half cooked scrambled eggs. With one hand on the handle and the other wielding a spatula, she didn't even care that her haphazard stirring was going to result in an unevenly cooked meal. She just wanted to get through one more lackluster breakfast and get the kids off to the store, where she would complete another week's worth of shopping while struggling to maintain order as she pushed the cart down the aisle.

More often than not, she found herself desperately trying to focus on finishing just one more thing, anything, without interruption; which meant striving with every ounce of her patience to ignore the tantrum unfolding at her feet. It started with Nathan, whose request to be held immediately turned into shrieks and screams when he did not get his way. She was used to this. "Hold on just a second, Nathan", she murmured tiredly into the eggs. But his shrieks didn't subside and soon they were joined by Eden who suddenly fell out of her chair at the kitchen table, knocking a fresh glass of milk to the floor in the process. Refusing to be ignored, their eldest, Titus, chimed in "Mom! Mom! Mom! Eden spilled her milk again! Look mom! Look!"

Evie broke.

Dropping the spatula into the hot skillet, she stormed out of the room and up the stairs, knocking Nathan to the floor not caring as she went. Slamming the bedroom door behind her, she rushed to the far side of the bed to get as far away as she could, fighting back the sobs of a desperate woman; desperate for a break, desperate for answers, desperate for the husband who was ripped from her without warning and who left a gaping hole in the heart of their home that couldn't be filled with time or pleas to God or anything within Evie's control. Then she heard Eden and Nathan, still crying, banging on the closed door with all of their might, needing her, demanding her, and ultimately sending her into the tears that she'd tried to fight back.

It wasn't their fault. They were her children, and she loved them. But it was happening more and more. The pressures of single parenthood on top of the grief and weight of unanswered questions surrounding Jonah's incarceration were wreaking havoc on her sanity. She sat down on the corner of her bed and placed her head in her hands as the sobs rolled out of her.

Eventually she stopped. The kids had quieted down and she heard the muffled sound of their giggles, happy again and playing together on the other side of the kitchen door. If only it were that simple for her. Tantrums and spilled milk were so easily fixed and forgotten compared to the weight she carried daily on her shoulders.

After staring blankly at a fray in the rug under her feet for what might have been a minute or an hour, her gaze was drawn to a large oil painting hanging on the wall on the opposite side of the room. It was her painting. For just a moment, her mind went back to its setting; the ornate, ivy covered red brick chapel that she and Jonah were married in. Painting hadn't been something she'd had time for in years, but she couldn't help but forget the world around her in this fleeting moment and admire her work. She looked at the clock on the face of the chapel's steeple, which read 6pm; the time of their wedding ceremony. She'd painted it in painstaking detail, wanting to honor that sacred day and time. But as her eyes moved outward from that clock, the landscape around the chapel became hazier. Farther from the clock, the less defined her brushstrokes became. Soon, they only hinted at the lush greenery surrounding the church on that warm June evening. Then her eyes drifted down to a large black shadow she'd painted in the foreground. She'd added a faint outline of two figures in the center of that shadow; her and Jonah walking together, hand in hand, just as they had after the ceremony was finished.

Suddenly, she snapped out of her brief trance as reality came rushing back. How ironic that their shadowy outlines hidden in the midst of a dark hole on an otherwise bright and cheerful painting would be all that was left of their marriage. Maybe everyone was right. Maybe it was better for her to move on. Forget Jonah ever existed. Relegate him to a hazy shadow of her past and start over. There could be freedom in that.

But even that small, soothing hope of release was taken from her just as soon as it was given. The relative silence was broken by Titus as he called to her from the kitchen, "Mom! Something smells weird in here!"

Turning her head back to the direction of her children, she remembered two things. One, the eggs were still cooking along with the spatula she'd hastily thrown into the skillet. She could smell the burnt eggs and melting rubber from where she sat. Second, those were Jonah's children in there. No matter how hard she might try to forget him, as if there was any chance she could truly bring herself to move on, his children would never let her forget. Their children. No, she could never stop fighting for Jonah.

With renewed resolve, she stood up, wiped her eyes, and walked back toward the kitchen, toward the charred mess on the stove and toward her beloved children who reminded her who she was, who Jonah was, and what she had to do next.

CHAPTER 5

Fingers crossed, Steve and Amy Jones huddled around the small TV. Usually he didn't play the lottery, but after being out of a job for the last year he started playing monthly. The prize: a one-way-all expenses-paid trip to Mars for you and your family as part of a recruiting gimmick by Unicore Technologies and Mining.

With the economy in shambles as a result of years of war, jobs and industry followed suit. Over-population in major cities, a nearly twenty percent unemployment, and failed attempts at rejuvenating the struggling economy made it easier for large companies to regroup on Mars, utilizing cheap labor from the skilled, but jobless, here on Earth. To play the lottery, you had to qualify: only those who had job experience (in Steve's case it was mining), were unemployed for over six months, and those no longer eligible to receive unemployment, could play. Steve and his family also easily passed the mandatory medical examinations that ensured that potential candidates were fit for the seven month journey. When Steve realized he could apply for the job in the form of the lottery, he jumped at the idea. If Mars was anything like the commercials and promotional videos on Unicore's website, he knew his wife and daughter would love it.

To the background of police sirens and arguing, Steve and Amy huddled close to the small TV in their two bedroom apartment. The numbers slowly appeared on the screen as a beautiful brunette woman in a beige Unicore dress read them aloud.

"Tonight's numbers are…Twenty-two…Fifteen…Seventeen"

Amy's eyes got wide. She looked at Steve.

"Seventeen again," said the announcer. "Have we ever had two seventeens in a row, John?

"No, I don't think so Scarlett," her host responded. "This must be a very lucky draw."

"And the last number is… TWENTY-ONE!"

Steve couldn't believe it. He read and reread the numbers at least three times over. Amy sat in awe, and then finally started to scream.

"We WON. We won Steve! We won!"

Steve stared blankly at the TV. *There is no way we could be this lucky. No way. I never win anything.*

The lady on the screen continued. "John, do we have the name?"

"We sure do Scarlett. Let's give a big round of applause to the newest Unicore employee Steve Jones!"

They hugged. Steve truly couldn't believe it. He'd go to the Unicore booth in the morning and turn in his ticket. *Finally, a break. My big break,* Steve thought.

CHAPTER 6

It stunk. The smell of burnt flesh hung low in the cold winter air. Blood stained the snow red as he wandered from his armored vehicle. A dispute over mineral rights in the Chukchi Sea instigated an all-out war between the US and Russia. Jonah had once again found himself in the middle of the conflict; but this time they were fighting Russian separatists on their own soil. Supplied by Russia, the separatists in western Alaska were well trained and properly equipped.

The improvised explosive device hidden under the snow was impossible to see until the flash of the explosion enveloped him. Jonah staggered away from his burning vehicle and fell to his knees. The snow was cold, but he couldn't feel it. A sense of calm surrounded him and the surge of adrenaline caused everything to move in slow motion. He looked around but couldn't quite focus on anything. Smoke rose from his armored vehicle, rays of the setting sun pierced a sky of iron colored clouds, men's voices shouted in the distance, and sounds of gunfire just barely louder than the ringing in his ears cracked past his head. A complex ambush. Armored vehicles pulled up to his right and returned fire. Jonah felt two men drag him onto the hood of a truck.

Despite its brutality, Jonah was good at war. It made sense to him. War wasn't as so many believed - just a group of apes slaughtering each other. There was purpose, strategy, desire. In war, you could see precisely what it was that drove men to do what they did; and those things that drove them were simple - love, fear, and anger. War had a way of breaking men down to their most basic states, and building them together as a team; as a form of art that rivaled Picasso or Van Gogh. Most of all, war wasn't pointless. Rebels under an intelligent leader could cripple an army and ruin an empire. Conversely, a brilliant military strategist could divide a rebellion without firing a single shot and destroy it from the inside out. Casualties were inevitable. But so was war it seemed.

Deep underground in a federal prison that had long been forgotten, Jonah prepared himself for his trial. The state had appointed a lawyer to serve on his behalf but they had barely met. It was clear to Jonah that they viewed his case as hopeless, or if not hopeless, it was bad business to try and defend one accused of treason by the state. Perhaps a decade ago, things would be different, but a lot had changed in the nation he once so eagerly defended. Now, to defend someone against charges levied by the state meant defiance of the state. Many defense attorneys refused to take on those cases, and the ones that did often found themselves bullied and marginalized for the remainder of their careers. Those accused of treason were left to fend for themselves, given only the pretense of a lawyer in the form of a state-financed public defender.

With no reading or writing materials provided him, Jonah's preparation consisted entirely of reciting what he had believed to be a convincing story. He would not lie and he would not quibble. But, if he could convince the judge that he was uninvolved in the suspected plot against the state rather than a planner and participant, he would do all that he could to convince them. Evie and their children were too important to play politics with. He did believe, however, that the key to protecting them was to ensure they all lived under a fair and transparent government, one which Jonah did not believe currently existed.

To pass the time, Jonah did push-ups and sit-ups, always reciting his defense as he did them. He never once saw his fellow prisoners and the guards never let them out for recess. In this prison, the inmates were deemed too dangerous to allow them any contact with each other or with the guards. The only sunlight came daily when the officials would open vents to allow fresh air down to the subterranean holding cell in an attempt to stem sickness that could easily sweep through the prison in a matter of hours.

Sweat dripped from his forehead onto the concrete below as he pushed through his final set of squats. Despite almost 12 years of fighting and six months in prison, his health was still superb. Scars had disappeared and injuries that required surgery had healed. None of this, of course, was natural. During the war in Russia, Jonah was unknowingly subjected to an experimental gene enhancement study under the guise of malaria-prevention medication. After the war, a whistle-blower exposed the whole experiment to the media and the program was terminated. Many senior white house officials went to jail and the gene enhancement studies ceased. Jonah was handed a large sum of money and was honorably discharged. Because of the controversy, there was no follow-up after his discharge to determine if the therapy had worked, and because only a handful of soldiers were actually exposed to the therapy, the leadership thought it was less dangerous to ignore any potential results and push everything under the rug.

For a while after the therapy, Jonah and Evie worried about everything. Were their unborn children at risk? What were the side effects? Had it even worked at all? Years later, Jonah determined that it had. The changes were subtle at first, but had recently erupted with odd yet wonderful changes. Jonah was stronger, faster, and far more durable. His body could function on less food and sleep while still performing beyond that of an Olympic athlete, with little focused exercise or training. While Jonah enjoyed the benefits, he was certain they would result in some form of cancer that had never been seen before. And so, without any certainty yet no need to go to the doctor, Jonah had simply attempted to eat healthy, exercise, and remain quiet. Even now, after being locked away for so long, Jonah could feel his strength in ways he could never possibly explain, and if he was going to be honest with himself, it felt good.

Jonah recited his statement once more and let his mind wander to the trial, the jury, and the judge as he completed his last repetition of squats. His defense was weak and he desperately hoped that the prosecution simply didn't have the evidence that he had done anything wrong. If he was going to be honest with himself, however, he knew he had walked a thin line between collaborating with an active rebellion while remaining neutral. This is the thing that tormented him the most - his actions directly led to his imprisonment, and the ones that suffered most were his wife and children.

With little airflow through the concrete passageways, sweat refused to evaporate and instead ran down his muscular arms, dripping into a small puddle on the cement floor below. He desperately craved water but the prison contained no fountain. Part of the guard's strategy was to keep their inmates only partially hydrated to ensure they never had all of their strength. He would have to wait until dinner to get his allotted glass. At first, this bothered him more than anything else about the small concrete and iron room. Over time, however, Jonah learned to control his thirst just as he had done everything else in his life - with hope. Jonah heartily hoped that there would be an end to all of this soon. All he had to do was be patient.

CHAPTER 7

Street lights danced lazily off the damp city streets as Evie covered the one mile stretch of pavement between the local convenience store and her home on the north side of town. While Jonah typically was the one to go on emergency supply runs, the job fell to Evie since his imprisonment. Walking briskly, she carried a single bag containing children's Tylenol for Nathan and cough syrup for herself. The fall had come early this year, and with it, all the colds a kid could catch.

Evie rarely left the home after dark. It simply wasn't safe anymore. The city she once joyfully explored, arm in arm with her husband and protector, was now a foreboding place. The dim glow of the street lights cast shadows across the sidewalk and the gentle breeze forced leaves and trash to tumble down the largely empty streets. She passed a gasoline and hydrogen station that had closed for the night, and most of the grocery shops contained lifeless interiors with metal bars shut against their entries. It wasn't just Evie who avoided going out at night.

A car light from behind reflected off a window causing her to spin around. She had been on edge since leaving the grocery store. *How far had she walked? A quarter of a mile, maybe half?* This was familiar terrain, but the night had a way of masking her ability to tell exactly where she was in relation to home. It was as if the night itself had draped a damp sheet over the city in an attempt to frustrate her senses. Perhaps it was simply the darkness that left her wary, but she couldn't help but suspect there was more. The street was never as dead as it was on this night. The gentle breeze continued to whistle and nudge at objects all around her, causing them to rustle in protest from being shoved about.

Evie looked over her shoulder again. *Was someone following her?* She looked forward but then did a double take behind her in the hopes of catching someone. No one could be seen. It was just the night playing with her eyes. *This was a different city in recent days.*

The war with Russia had a devastating effect on the nation. What started as a war over resources became a global conflict, forcing the European Union to take sides with the United States while the Alliance of Arab States sided with Russia. Oil and natural gas exports sunk, but the worst was yet to come. Under the assumption that a crippling blow to Arab oil and gas exports would force Russia to reenter negotiations and subdue the fighting, the European Union launched a series of attacks against oil and gas production centers and transportation pipelines across the Arab Alliance.

What was meant to be a crippling blow to Russia's only ally instead incited greater violence and an all-out conventional war by the Russians. Using bombers followed by a ground invasion into Eastern Europe, Russian forces advanced quickly and conquered large swaths of land. Faced with the destruction of major western cities, American bombers resorted to a last ditch, terrain-denial offensive effort by literally irradiating thousands of miles of land from Poland to the Black Sea.

The effects on the environment were devastating, but the effects on the global stage were even worse. With Russia reeling from casualties and Europe struggling to sustain itself, China saw an opportunity to seize the much needed resources that the Arab Alliance had struggled to defend. The nation marched several million soldiers from Pakistan all the way to the Mediterranean Sea and further irradiated their own borders between Russia and Europe.

Finally, the three remaining nations had seen enough bloodshed and signed a truce. Evie remembered how relieved she was when Jonah returned from the fighting in Eastern Russia but the end of the armed conflict only sent Russia, China, and the United States into a second Cold War with the stakes much higher. The government soon began using fear and intimidation as a method to search for foreigners acting as spies. They instituted a curfew and staged high profile arrests in broad daylight; but with so much of the government budget focused on external threats, the nation itself became rife with organized crime. Begging for more protection, citizens voted for more regulations and politicians consolidated power in the executive branch in order to make and execute decisions much faster. Eventually, security returned and the economy was stabilized, but the cost to the average citizen was monumental. Living in the shell of democracy, a fragile totalitarian state began to take its shape.

Evie turned left off the main street and stopped. A car was parked just a few hundred meters down the road with its lights off. She could see the shadows of two men inside. *It's probably nothing*, she reminded herself. But she couldn't be sure. While those guys were most likely waiting for a friend, they were just as likely to be waiting for an unsuspecting passerby. Evie retraced her steps and decided to continue walking up the main drag. She would cut in at the next corner and loop back around.

The cool fall air ripped through her jacket as she strode quickly up the hill. Behind her she could hear a vehicle start. Certain it was the car from the side road, Evie broke into a jog. Just as she could see car lights reflecting off the wet pavement she dodged onto the side road and ducked underneath an entryway awning. Evie squeezed her body flush against the closed bakery shop door. She didn't breath. She couldn't. The car slowly drove past the street and pulled into an empty roadside parking space just ahead of her. Evie stepped from her hiding spot and jogged the rest of the way home. She made up her mind. When Jonah's trial was over, they were all going to move south.

CHAPTER 8

The Jones' house was a mess. In the last two weeks they had sold and given away everything they could, but with only two weeks left, the task before them seemed daunting.

Steve rushed about frantically. "Amy! Where's the car title?"

"I don't know Steve," Amy called back from a different room, busy pulling clothes out of the closet to give to the local thrift store.

"Damn it, Amy! I asked you to find that last week," Steve shouted back. He was frustrated. Sometimes he felt like he had to do everything himself. He'd never say it out loud, but this family was dragging him down. Recently, Steve found himself wondering if he'd be better off doing things on his own. Of course, because of the trip to Mars, it was too late now, but he firmly believed sacrifice had to be a family effort. Steve couldn't just shoulder the whole burden himself, *could he?* Frustrated and burdened, Steve stormed into the kitchen, opening and slamming drawers looking for the title.

****

Amy knew to stay in the bedroom when he got like this. Even though Steve had never been abusive to them he certainly had a temper. Steve never said it, but Amy always suspected he lost his job because of his temper, not his skills. The mining community was close-knit and talked about its employees. When someone was let go, the rest of the community knew why. In Amy's mind, he was fired because of his temper and was later stonewalled by other employers for the same reason. No one wants to work with someone who so easily blew a gasket at the drop of a hat.

Shaking her head and hoping the new job would relieve some of his stress, Amy pulled another swath of clothes from the closet, uncovering her wedding dress. After all these years, it remained neatly hung in the same spot. She found herself wondering if she could still fit into it, but knew she didn't have the time to try. Besides, if by some chance Steve came back and found her doing anything but packing, he wouldn't be happy. They couldn't take it to Mars. She pulled it off the hanger and folded it into the box. Amy couldn't help but tear up. The dress was only the start. Photos, albums, and keepsakes. All of it had to stay. It was tough, and truthfully, she didn't want to go – but she would follow Steve anywhere – after all, sacrifice was a family affair, and everyone would give equally.

CHAPTER 9

Evie warmed herself by the courtyard fire; it was another cold night for October. She stared into the flames as they danced back and forth. Sparks jumped off logs and disappeared into the night. The elongated shadows of two military guards stretched across the entrance to the military tribunal. Evie had not seen her husband for six months. For six months she had called congressmen, written senators, and wept hopelessly at night. Her prayers to God had never been more genuine. And yet they remained unanswered.

Evie was forced to handle this ordeal alone and she was terrified the trial would not bring any resolution to her nightmare. *War crimes? How could he possibly be accused of war crimes?* She knew Jonah, and she knew he would not kill innocent people. Her husband wasn't a monster; he was a wonderful father and an honorable man. But no one would listen, and so, in the dark cold night she stood there.

Fog hung low in the air. Its wispy fingers stretched out along the walk, inching closer and closer to Evie. Flames jumped and the fingers parted, enveloping her on each side. They dared not come into the light.

For reasons unknown to everyone except those putting her husband on trial, Evie had been not allowed to take any part in his defense. She knew nothing of his accusers. Other than an assigned lawyer, who claimed he had signed a confidentiality agreement and was not able to discuss the case, she was completely and utterly in the dark. This total lack of information worried her far more than anything else. After several hours of waiting, a man exited the main door - the public lawyer the courts assigned the family. Exuding a sense of self-importance, he made his way to Evie. As he walked towards her, the fog parted but quickly swarmed back in his wake.

"I'm so sorry, Evie," he began.

Everything immediately got farther away. She could hear her heart beating in her chest. Her temples throbbed. *This can't be. What did he do? What will we do?*

He continued to talk, but she only caught bits and pieces. *Life in prison.* Her face felt hot. *Mars.* Black spots formed around her eyes. All at once it seemed the fire she stood by died and the fog rushed in on her, seizing this opportunity to overtake her soul.

"Evie?" the lawyer said gently. He gripped her arm breaking her panic. "Evie, Jonah wanted you to have this note." The man fished in his pocket, eventually producing a torn piece of paper. A note from Jonah.

Evie took the note from his hand and read it through her tear-blurred vision. It had been scribbled on a piece of legal paper torn off the lawyer's pad-

I will come back for you, Evie. I love you so much. ~ Jonah.

Hours passed but Evie remained frozen, tethered to her spot by the fire in front of her and to her husband somewhere behind the compound's walls. Although she shivered, she couldn't feel the cold. Although the fire blazed next to her, she didn't notice. *There had to be something she could do. She would not turn her back on Jonah, not now, and not ever.* She gripped the note harder in her hand and made a pledge that only her heart could understand. And with that she turned from the fire and started for her car. Eventually, Evie went home. With the kids already in bed, she paid their babysitter, went upstairs, and cried until she fell asleep.

CHAPTER 10

The meetings had picked up recently. They had to. In the last few months, they had seen the federal Government issue an unnerving number of arrest warrants and edicts. Most red state senators no longer traveled to the capital to conduct their business and instead opted to vote by proxy. In some states, namely Texas and Arizona, the state governments even established border checkpoints to help identify any federal agents crossing into their territory.

In the basement of the government building sat a delegation of fifty-two men and women from all the states. With a few minutes left before the meeting, John went through his notes one last time, while halfheartedly listening to the sidebar conversations around him. He could hear one particularly lively conversation, with one delegate claiming "It's not like we can just go to war with them!"

John raised his hand and cleared his throat. As the meeting's speaker, he was ready to begin.

"Let the assembly of the Free States be silent for roll call," his voice boomed into the microphone placed at the end of his cherry stained podium at the front of the room.

The clerk, with paper and pen crouched over a small desk in the back began, "Alaska... Idaho... Montana... North Dakota... South Dakota... Wyoming... Nebraska... Utah... Arizona... Texas... Oklahoma... Kansas... Missouri..." each state representative raised his or her hand and said present.

"Arkansas... Louisiana... Mississippi... Indiana... Alabama... Tennessee... Kentucky... Indiana... West Virginia... Virginia... Alabama... Georgia... South Carolina..., and lastly, North Carolina."

The clerk looked back at the honorable John Wilkes from Virginia. "Mr. Wilkes, the assembly is formed and present."

John then took over the floor again.

"Thank you all for coming. It is the pleasure of the people of Richmond, Virginia to welcome you to our great city for such an important meeting. As you have already been made aware, we will be reviewing our grievances with the federal government and putting final touches on our list of both grievances and demands. This article will be titled "Grievances Against a Totalitarian State" and will be sent to every major newspaper, as well as to congressmen and senators on both sides. I would ask all of you to be patient as I read through the list, and then we can address specific grievances to tailor, add to, or remove completely. Let's begin:

"Grievance one: Increased federal taxes levied against states not in compliance with certain executive orders.

Two: Illegitimate resource-driven declarations of war against sovereign nations without congressional approval.

Three: Illegal and overarching executive powers nullifying the previously established system of checks and balances.

Four: The encouraged and federally rewarded practice of eugenics and abortions based on economic, social, or a physical disability status.

The list continued, and once he stopped reading, the arguing ensued. Some states wanted grievances added, while others wanted some taken away. By the end of the meeting, the council had agreed to fifteen grievances and all twenty-seven governors signed their name to the list. Above their signature was the following statement:

"We, the Free States of the United States of America, present this list of grievances against a totalitarian state. We refuse to comply with the accompanying mandates laid out in the above list and laws associated with grievances in the above list. No longer will the Free States pay taxes to the Federal Government, nor will the Free States allow federal law enforcement to enforce the laws in those states that have signed below. We urge the federal government and all remaining states not currently in our assembly to engage us diplomatically over these matters."

As the governor of Tennessee approached the table to sign, he looked at John and sighed. His eyes were soft and his face was weathered.

"John, you know the federal government will never accept this."

"I know," John replied, faking a thin smile.

"Then you agree. This will, without a doubt, lead to a war that further divides the nation."

"Yes, Ted, I agree."

"We're going to need to start planning this in public – so the people fully understand what we've signed them up for."

John nodded, "They already understand. But we're going to need a spokesperson that people can rally behind, all the same."

"You're a border state, John. Are you sure you're ready if the Federalists attack?"

"We have been acting as two separate nations for so long now," he said warily with a sigh. "Our generals are with us, and our border has never been stronger."

"We lost a lot when we lost Jonah, didn't we?" Ted asked, looking at the floor now as if he was ashamed to mention his name without paying respect.

"Yes..." John trailed off, not certain how to further respond. They had lost more than he could put into words.

CHAPTER 11

"The car's here! Hurry!" exclaimed Steve.

They were all set. Their bags were packed, their cars had finally been sold, and the apartment was as empty of furniture as his fishing pond was empty of fish; which, coincidentally, is exactly what Steve suspected about his fishing pond. Only once did Steve get something to nibble on his hook in over a year of fishing, but when he reeled it in, there was nothing but the shrewd remains of a waterlogged stick. Regardless, Steve's luck had just changed. He had even rented a classy town car with all the upgrades using his last few Earth dollars to shuttle them to the airport. Now for the most difficult task of all — getting two women out of the house on time.

"Amy, let's go; that ship will leave without us! Have you seen

Zoe? Just put your bags near the door, I'll carry them out. Let's go, Zoe, the car's here!"

Amy didn't want her last thought on Earth to be her nervous husband rushing them to and fro, but it didn't look like she had a choice. Before she could answer him, Steve was already moving bags to the car. She went to Zoe's room to move her along.

"Are you ready to go, honey?" Amy asked tenderly. She couldn't imagine what her 14 year old daughter must be experiencing right now. It's something you never could prepare for.

Zoe was sitting, leaned up against the far wall of her empty room. Sunlight from the only window shined against her face in such a way that made Amy take a step back. She was so young and full of life, promise, and potential. Amy couldn't help but wonder if they were doing the right thing. "What will Mars be like, mom?" Zoe asked. Of course, she knew what Mars would be like; she had watched all the same videos they did. But the question was important all the same. Zoe had grown up in the same home, in the same town, surrounded by the same friends for fourteen years. The question wasn't about what it would physically be like. The question was deeper. Will we make friends? Will I enjoy it? What if I don't? Amy had asked the same questions countless times; yet, she didn't have an answer to give. Not a real one anyway.

Amy crouched down and put a hand on Zoe's knee. "You're going to love it honey. Now let's go before your dad freaks out more than he already is." Amy winked and pulled Zoe to her feet, through the mottled blue hallway, out of the red front door, down the concrete stairs with a black iron banister, and into the black town car. To Zoe, it looked like a hearse.

CHAPTER 12

From behind the glass, she writhed in agony. Her face drizzled with beads of sweat. She opened her mouth to scream but nobody could hear the words she said. The microphone had been turned off. Her fingernails desperately clawed at her face and hair. Finding a corner, she curled up and wept.

The two looked on from the other side of the safety glass. "Why don't you think it worked?" one asked the other. The other shrugged. "I'm not sure we understand the human body as much we had hoped." Soon, the girl was writhing again. She grimaced, showing her teeth as she pulled at the loosely fitted gown that draped over her body.

"How much longer do you want to watch this?" the second

asked the first.

"It's like she was poisoned." The first observed. "Everyone we've tried, regardless of the changes we make, have the same outcome. They all seem poisoned." She paused. "Was there anything alive in there? Anything at all?"

"There wasn't."

The woman went to walk out and then turned back around to the window just in time to watch the girl's eyes roll back in her head as she passed out from the pain. "Put her out of her misery. Make sure we do a good autopsy. Focus on toxicology; especially in her blood. We're getting another one soon – a completely different one. Keep your fingers crossed that this will be the one."

She turned again and walked out. Her partner stood there for another minute, staring blankly at the girl on the floor in the bright concrete room. Whenever they lost someone, he couldn't help but feel bad – not guilty, just bad. It was hard watching them endure such pain. But in order for society to progress forward, it required sacrifice. He was certain these people would be remembered as pioneers when they finally got it right. And get it right they would. It just took time. The girl began to wake up again, but this time, instead of letting her endure even more pain than she already had, he lifted a cover revealing a grey switch. Flipping it with his index finger, he removed all the oxygen from the chamber – it literally sucked the life from her and left her body lifeless on the floor.

CHAPTER 13

Inside, the Unicore spaceship was vast. The white seats looked more like eggs, wrapping fully around its occupant, and reclined fully to the ground. Unlike an airplane, the seats lined the walls of the space ship and faced inward. The aisle had a brightly lit walkway down the center leading to the pilot's cabin in one direction and the exit ramp in the other. Halfway down the corridor was an exit hatch nestled securely to the floor. Between each seat was an armrest but it was larger and formed a bit of a cocoon around the occupant. Above was a face mask with cords and wires coming out of it.

"What's this for?" Zoe asked the stewardess.

"It's a long flight sweetie; once we get out of Earth's

atmosphere we're all going to go to sleep. This mask helps," She replied, continuing her checks through the cabin.

"Daddy, is it just us?"

"I don't know hon, here, put your seatbelt on."

The ship was huge and could have easily carried several hundred people, but it remained empty. What a waste of space Zoe thought.

As if on cue, the clanking of chains up the loading ramp echoed off the interior cabin walls. All three looked down the ramp, while the stewardess pretended to be unaware of any strange noise.

Escorted by two grey-suited guards, Jonah walked slowly down the aisle. His feet and hands were shackled together, and he wore a grilled face mask over his head. The guards brought him to within a few seats of Zoe on the opposite side and sat him down.

"Daddy," Zoe whispered in a voice that was closer to shouting than whispering. "Who's that?"

"I don't know," Steve whispered back. "Just ignore him."

"What's on his face," she continued, intending to be quiet but once again making enough noise to startle a scarecrow.

Steve did his best to ignore her last question, but Amy leaned across his chest and continued to dialog about the extremely dangerous looking man sitting almost directly across from them.

"It's a shield to prevent him from biting the guards," she replied.

At the thought of this large man restrained in chains trying to bite his way to freedom, Zoe let out a giggle. But when she looked up at him to affirm the humor of the situation she stopped. His face was in complete shadow behind the mask, and he easily towered over the two men escorting him. She imagined him watching her and shuddered.

The guards finished locking Jonah into his seat and began to walk off.

"Excuse me!" Steve piped up to one of them. "There are tons of seats on this ship; why did you have to put him directly across from us?"

The guards looked at each other, shrugged, and kept walking off the ship. One looked to his partner and said something that caused them both to laugh.

Steve couldn't believe it. Looking around again, he found the stewardess. "Miss, can you have him moved to a different seat?"

"I'm sorry sir; there aren't any guards on board to move him. We're going to put you all to sleep very soon, and you won't see him again."

Steve wasn't comforted.

CHAPTER 14

Even in his deepest despair, Jonah couldn't help but marvel. Here he sat, on his way to be buried and forgotten inside a Martian prison, and directly across from him was a family that had just won the lottery - also heading to Mars. His nightmare and their dream.

He had to focus now. Evie and the kids were too important to him to never see them again. The note he'd asked his lawyer to pass Evie was simple, but he intended to honor it. Many times when Jonah would go to training or to war, he found himself wishing there would be a problem with his aircraft. That he would get one more day with his family. That somehow, even the most miniscule delay would mean the deployment was cancelled altogether. Every time, he left without the miracle he had hoped for. Now, more than ever, he hoped for that miracle. Yet in his deepest thoughts, he knew no miracle would come.

I will come back for you. The trip to Mars might as well have been the death penalty. To live out the rest of his life in a prison cell, on an alien planet where he would receive no letters, no phone calls, and no visits was worse than death. His country had abandoned him. They sold him out on false charges during a sham trial in the middle of the night. He said it to himself one more time; a pledge. *I will come back for you, Evie.*

Just then the stewardess interrupted his thoughts.

"Sir, we are authorized to remove your face guard now that you are restrained in your seat. Understand that this is so that you can wear the mask that will help you fall asleep during the trip." She paused. "Should you cause a disturbance or spit at our guests we will put your face mask back on and you will sit here for the next five months doing nothing. Do you agree to behave?" she asked.

Jonah nodded. *Did prisoners really forego the face mask just to spit at a few people? If they did, he was certain they regretted their decision within the first day of flight.*

Pulling a small silver key from a side pocket on her black and green jumpsuit, the young woman inserted and turned the key into a lock along his jaw line. He could feel the mask loosen and pressure instantly came off his chin and teeth. He closed his eyes and breathed gently. For the first time in six months, someone had just treated him like a human. Although she didn't touch him, he imagined he felt her warm hand gently rest on his shoulder. Jonah's eyes teared up. He kept them closed tight.

Why is God doing this to me? Jonah thought. *This is more than I can bear.*

Jonah opened his eyes to see the girl across from him staring. He looked down at the ground. Jonah's stomach ached. His chest hurt. He felt defeated. *This is more than I can bear.*

The ship began to rumble as its four engines revved violently. Jonah felt the ship lurch forward as its pilot released the brakes. Through the small porthole he could see the ship turn to taxi towards the main runway. Runway lights illuminated the ground, and lights from the city cast a halo against the darkening sky. The ship accelerated abruptly as it hit the main runway and he could feel his shoulder pressing hard against the side of his egg shell seat. Soon they were off, the city lights left behind them as they shot down the airstrip and hurtled out of the atmosphere at an incredible rate of speed.

"Look at that, mom!" shouted Zoe, pointing out the window.

A circle surrounding the Earth glowed with a majestic blue green on one side of the horizon while the setting sun cascaded oranges and reds off the other. City lights in the night sky burned a pumpkin orange, and the busy highways were illuminated with streaks of blurred whites and reds from head and tail lights as cars raced home from work. Before he could truly take it all in, they were past Earth and there was nothing but the black void of space.

Soon the stewardess came around and began pushing buttons to recline the beds and store the ship's passengers away for the flight. As she depressed the button, the egg chairs unfolded and reclined toward the ground, forming a six foot cocoon around its occupant. As she reached Steve's chair he looked perplexed.

"Why do the chairs cover you completely?"

"When we leave the Earth's magnetic field, we'll all be exposed to dangerous radiation from the sun," she promptly responded. "These chairs are built with protective material to absorb and reflect the radiation."

"The whole ship doesn't have that protection?" He asked.

"It's cheaper and lighter this way," She said with a smile, as she began pushing his button.

Steve looked appalled at that answer. Jonah thought he could hear some muttering about cutting costs and cheap manufacturing but he wasn't sure. After putting the family down, she finally made it to Jonah.

"Sir, I'm going to help you put this mask around your face. Are you willing to cooperate?"

Jonah could tell she was cautious but not necessarily nervous; as if she wasn't convinced he would try to bite her hand off, but conventional wisdom still dictates that you avoid putting your fingers through the cage at a zoo. He was a criminal to everyone. Barely human – no better than a savage animal.

"I'm innocent," Jonah said, doing his best to make eye contact in the least intimidating way possible.

"I know," she replied. "They don't send the guilty to Mars

anymore."

She gently put the mask over his face. Jonah wasn't sure if that was just a standard line she gave or if she believed him, but he had to ask his follow up question regardless. "Will you help me?" he asked.

"When I move you to your landing vessel, I've been instructed to put the key in your pod. That's all I can do," She said quietly.

The mask had already started to take effect and Jonah wasn't sure if he had heard her right. He fought the gasses' effects, desperately trying to make sense of her comments in his head. He dreamily wondered who ordered her to leave the key for his chains but could no longer muster the energy to care. Suddenly he realized it had been Mickey Mouse that ordered the key hung above his head, but that didn't sound right either, and with the same spontaneity that the thought entered his mind, Mickey Mouse and his crew of jolly animals departed as if they were on the set of a Broadway musical. His thoughts dwelled on the peculiarity for only a moment longer before returning to Evie and the kids. *I'll come back for you Evie*, he thought. This was the easiest he'd fallen asleep in a long time.

CHAPTER 15

Evie could see her footprints on the snow blanketed sidewalk leading up to the capitol building. The snow was wet and heavy. At times, fierce gusts of wind pushed the thick wet flakes into her face and knocked clumps off the rows of trees that lined her path.

Evie's heart was heavy. She kept her shoulders rolled forward reflecting the burden of the stress she'd been under for the last few months. Thanksgiving, Christmas, and the New Year were a depressing blur. Even though she had sent her husband off before, there was always the promise of return. This time, he had been taken without even allowing her family a moment to say goodbye.

Friends faked pity, and after a while, family did their best to pretend that nothing was wrong – as if somehow she was just supposed to move on with her life. Even through their veiled acts of kindness, she knew that under the circumstances, no one really expected Jonah to return. Impatiently, everyone was asking her to do the same thing. Move on. Forget the father of her children and husband of her youth. Sometimes she truly wanted to. Sometimes she longed for companionship so deeply that the very sight of other couples laughing together and holding each other left her hopeless and distraught. Sometimes, she even encouraged herself to move on.

When push came to shove, however, she couldn't do that. She wouldn't do that. And so, she pressed on. Congressmen and senators all pretended to be sorry, but did nothing. The military stopped returning her calls. Everyone was stonewalling her. One governor even had the gall to tell her to forget that she was ever married to Jonah, and she would do best to move on with her life. Evie ignored them, faithfully pursuing a means to her husband's return. As she continued her trek, she was taken farther and farther south. Jonah had fought so hard and sacrificed so much for this country – she was determined to do the same for him.

Finally, at an invitation in the mail, she arrived at the State Capitol building in Richmond, Virginia. Two armed guards met her at the large doors and led her into the lobby. After passing through a metal detector, she was seated on a black leather couch. The building was beautifully decorated with large stone columns and a thirty foot ceiling. The windows were dressed in stained glass and elegant flowing drapes. The floor was black and white tiled marble and in a seal embedded in the center was a woman wrapped in blue holding a spear. Below the woman were the words *SIC SEMPER TYRANNIS.*

After some time, an older gentlemen with a southern accent came out to greet her. He smiled big and extended his hand graciously.

"Evangeline, so great to finally meet you!"

"Hi, thank you, and you can call me Evie," she responded as he led her back to his office. "What does the seal mean?"

"The seal?"

"Yes, the seal on the lobby floor?"

"Oh," he exclaimed, smiling at her. "Thus, always, to tyrants — it's a Latin phrase, Evie. It literally means 'Thus always I eradicate tyrants' lives.' We think it's quite fitting for our noble state, don't you?"

Evie nodded, repeating what he said in her mind, trying to determine what he really meant. Making their way down the long corridor, they arrived at a nicely furnished office. He closed the door behind them and offered her some tea.

"Please Evie, sit down and make yourself comfortable."

She sat, but she wasn't comfortable. *What was his angle?* Of all the congressmen she solicited help from, not one was willing to help; save for the governor of Virginia, Mr. Wilkes. Evie looked around trying to soak everything in. His desk was a large deep cherry color bracketed on each side with bookshelves loaded with more books than a single person could hope to read in a lifetime.

The windows, large and luxurious, offered a stunning view of the city below, and a small table in the corner near the door she had just entered supported a coffee maker and clear glass mugs. Mr. Wilkes himself wore a black suit with a red and blue striped tie attached to a plain white shirt. He removed his jacket as he sat and gave her a brief smile.

"Evie, I have to be frank with you." He started, pushing a glass of tea towards her from behind his desk. "The situation you've found yourself in isn't uncommon."

She was startled. *What do you mean, isn't uncommon? Do many innocent men who've served their countries with honor find themselves guilty before proven innocent and betrayed; cast out on a one way mission to Mars?*

"Unfortunately," he continued, "we've seen a good number of our citizens jailed lately. Largely on circumstantial or even entirely falsified evidence." He paused. "Evie, did Jonah ever tell you about his interactions with us?"

Evie was caught off guard. "Interactions?"

He looked around the room and finally found what he was searching for, a small cassette player, and turned it on. Classical music softly filled the room.

Governor Wilkes leaned towards her and spoke more softly. "Evie, you've seen the news, yes?"

She nodded.

"The fact is, there has been some significant disagreement between the federal government and the states in recent years." He paused again. "Evie, we asked your husband to consider advising us.

Militarily."

Evie couldn't believe what she was hearing. *A military? An army? He never said anything? How could he have kept this from me? Civil War? Is this what he was telling her? Civil War?*

Governor Wilkes remained silent. He was intuitive enough to know she was working through her thoughts.

"Mr. Wilkes, I don't understand... are you suggesting he was arrested for treason?"

John didn't respond, but instead took a sip of his own tea and continued to watch her apologetically.

"I can't believe this? Is it that bad? Why would he help start a civil war? How could you even bring him into this?" She was agitated, upset, and confused.

"I know this is hard to believe Evie," he started, "but please understand our position. Truth be told, your husband was more eager to help us than you might want to think. He believed in what we're doing."

Deep down, she knew that was the truth. Jonah was sick of the political climate and had talked openly more than a few times about the corruption he had seen in the government.

"Evie, Jonah believed in this very much. We think we can exploit what they did to him. With your testimony, and other proof we've collected, we think this can push the public in our favor. It would help explain one more case of the egregious actions the federal government has taken leading to our current opinion that diplomacy is no longer an option. Would you be willing to help us?"

"Yes," Evie said, before she realized she said it. But it was the truth. "If we win… will we be able to bring him back?"

Reaching across the desk he took her hands into his. "I promise you Evie, I will do everything I can to bring him back."

As she got up to leave, John stood as well and reached over to grab her arm. "Evie. It won't be safe for you and your children if you leave here for your home in the North. I've arranged for a home here in the city if you are willing to move."

She couldn't believe what she was hearing, but she decided, surprisingly, that she trusted him. He was the only one who had paid her any attention and offered to help bring her husband home. Whether or not she was making the right decision was irrelevant. She would continue to strive towards bringing Jonah back, and if this man could offer that, then this was where she would be. Evie nodded, and John smiled and let go of her arm. For the first time in months, Evie squared her shoulders and walked bravely from the office. She was finally making progress.

****

John watched her leave and walked over to his window. He couldn't help but stare into the stormy sky and wonder where Jonah was in his journey. He was closer to Jonah than he had led Evie to believe. Jonah had provided more than a small amount of insight into the strategy and doctrines of warfare. He had been a major figure in the construction of the grievances against the federal government and had been chosen to not simply advise their government, but to play a pivotal role in the defense of their new republic. To suggest that Governor Wilkes was not grieving the loss of Jonah couldn't have been further from the truth. John also failed to mention that there was an effort underway at this very moment to free Jonah. But it would take time. Time that he feared the new Federation of Free States did not have.

CHAPTER 16

"This food sucks!" Adiela complained, thrusting the mush on her fork back onto her tray.

"They're just mashed potatoes," replied her surprised and somewhat exasperated step-mother. "I don't know what's gotten into you honey. You've just been so difficult lately."

Adi wasn't sure if the accusation about her being difficult, or the Canadian accent of her step-mother that feigned surprise, was more atrocious. *How could she not know what's gotten into me?* "WE'RE ON MARS, KATHY!" she shouted loudly, flinging another scoop of the gulag potatoes onto the tray and garnering the looks of fellow diners from across the food court. "And if I eat another bowl of this crap I'm going to vomit!"

Adi's step-mother was a private woman and immediately looked down at the table while leaning in towards Adi. "Keep your voice down," she hissed. Adiela threw her fork against the tray and folded her arms in protest, leaning back in her chair and away from the sludge on her plate. Glaring up at her step-mother to demonstrate her disgust at the prospect of spending one more moment eating the gruesome plate of God-knows-what that this horrid camp attempted to pass as mashed potatoes, she saw only forehead and graying blond hair. Kathy was a professional when it came avoiding confrontation, and this time was no different. With her head down and a pleasant smile across her face, she only managed to infuriate Adi even more.

Not finding the battle she was hoping for with Kathy, Adiela looked around the metallic cafeteria hoping to lock eyes with another doomed member of this hellish Martian colony. A few people, some miners and some scientists, were watching her but glanced down as soon as she turned towards them. To Adi, the cafeteria looked like a hospital dining facility for the terminally ill. The tables and chairs had a metallic shine that screamed surgery or mortuary, the floors were a pale linoleum tile, and the ceilings beamed with bright lights. Even her tray reminded her of being in either a prison or a hospital. Any luster this place once held was gone, even the metallic shine on the table had been scraped and scratched dry from the countless number of meals.

Adi moved her hand from her tray to her arm to check the status of the small needle prick she received earlier this morning.

Apparently, whenever a new member of the colony arrived, the scientists had to draw blood to check for any infections that could put the rest of the colony at risk. Lifting the brown Band-Aid and small cotton swab revealed a dark red stain of blood. The spot itself looked much better and Adi decided her time would be better spent removing her dressing as opposed to eating the slop.

"Stop picking at yourself, Adi," insisted her stepmother, looking back down at her plate immediately to avoid any potential conflict or protest.

Adi begrudgingly obliged, crossed her arms against her chest and again looked around the room. This time she caught the eyes of a twenty-something pretty blond haired girl watching her. The girl didn't look down and instead returned her stare intently. Her blue eyes and deep red lips were always something that young Adiela admired, and she found herself compelled by her beauty. The look on her face, however, was one of deep sorrow. Adi found herself wondering just how long the woman had been here. Refusing to stare any longer, the woman in the checkered blue and black long sleeved shirt stood up and left with her tray. Adi looked back at Kathy. "When's dad supposed to get back?"

"I don't know… but we're meeting with Jillian when he does. You can watch a movie tonight until we get back."

Adi's father wasn't a miner, but he was hired by the company to perform maintenance on their drills. Although a skilled mechanic, he hadn't been able to find work on Earth, forcing the small family of just three to play the lottery and head to Mars in search of opportunity. While Adi hated leaving, she looked up to her father. He had worked hard to put food on their table, and early on, Adi found herself playing the role of homemaker without a mother to help. Where her mother was, he wouldn't say, but eventually Adiela learned to deal with the fact that she didn't have to know everything. She simply enjoyed the relationship they had together. At least she did until Kathy showed up.

The annoying accent that frequently barged into Adiela's mind and pulled her out of her thoughts once again charged from the mouth of the woman sitting across from her. "What'd you like to do after lunch? We could go through the shops behind the hotel." Adiela rolled her eyes but remained silent and hoped her stepmother would get the picture. She didn't. "Well, fine. If you are going to be difficult, you can find your own way back to the room. I'll be at the shops," she declared, scooting out her chair and walking away before Adi could say a word. Adiela sat for a moment longer continuing to survey the crowd. *Where are all the boys,* she wondered. It was bad enough that she was uprooted here, but now that she had time to see the other settlers, she realized they were nothing but fifty-year old couples and a few young women. Not a single boy her age. How on earth was she supposed to have fun here?!

Adi got up to dump her tray and spotted the young woman again. She was once again staring at Adiela, but this time nodded her head as if to say "come over here." Adi obliged.

CHAPTER 17

Hurtling silently through space, five passengers, two pilots, and a flight attendant slept peacefully. After putting their passengers to sleep, the crew traveled to the moon base and docked there for a month. To send four passengers to Mars without a secondary mission would have been an absurd waste of money. The travel itself was relatively cheap; the quantum propulsion engine, which had been developed a few years ago, was a money saver. But exiting the earth's atmosphere still required the high octane acceleration that only jet fuel could truly produce.

The ship and its crew unloaded precious life-sustaining cargo to the small moon outpost, added a passenger who was taking his rest and recovery on earth, and set out again for Mars. Now, over halfway through their journey the chemicals that had been pouring into the stewardess' mask turned off and a small red light began flashing in front of her eyes. It was dim at first, but it slowly increased in intensity until she began to rouse. Blinking once, and then twice, she reached up and turned a dial above her alcove to make the light white and initiate the sequence that raised her bed into a seat to allow her to conduct her checks. The three of them had a system when traveling towards Mars. Every month, one of them clambered out of their slumber and checked the ship and its systems for anything that could signal trouble.

With her chair fully raised, Jane paused a few more moments before getting up to walk around. While the gas contained special chemicals to reduce muscle atrophy, she still hadn't used them in months. Jane gently massaged her legs to get the blood flowing back into them and stimulate the muscles to prep them for work. Once, Jane had jumped out too quickly and found herself on the floor with a bloody nose. That was a sufficient lesson to remind Jane to take her time. After all... she had two more months and nowhere to go!

Finally, Jane slid from the seat and onto the metallic walkway. Her feet made a clang as they touched the steel grated walkway below and she felt the impact vibrate up through her entire body. Holding onto the chair to steady herself, she paused to make certain she could walk. The ship hummed gently as its engines continued to propel them towards their destination. Although not on the official list, that hum was always her first check. Are we stuck in space floating endlessly at a speed and on a course that will leave us in the deep cold to die, or does the ship still work? Jane was happy to check her mental block in the affirmative as she began walking towards the passenger section.

Although Jane was an attractive young woman, she had never wanted to settle down. She had watched her father and mother argue for most of her youth, until eventually separating. On the hard days as a young girl she would go outside and sit in the backyard, waiting for the fighting to stop. Jane could still remember looking up at the stars, wondering what it would be like to visit them. She paused at one of the windows and looked outside. The space beyond the porthole was black and lifeless. The stars she dreamt about as a child remained just as out of reach from space as they had while she was on earth. Fortunately, she was happy here nonetheless.

Jane continued walking down the aisle and stopped in front of the criminal's bed. He was handsome; tall and muscular, but he wasn't peaceful. Even as he was held in the chemically-induced sleep, the criminal moved and shook violently. His eyes twitched back and forth behind his eyelids and his hands clenched into fists, relaxing only to clench again. Jane had never seen such a thing. Typically, the chemicals put the traveler in such a deep sleep that they dreamed nothing, and their minds were so disconnected from the rest of their bodies they were incapable of moving.

Jane watched him a bit longer, perplexed. He appeared so tormented inside. She couldn't help but wonder what he had been through. For a minute, she felt pity, but as the feeling of pity was accompanied by an inability to do anything for the man, she decided to continue on - first checking the other passengers and then the computer systems. With her checks complete she wandered slowly back to her cocoon to rest just a little longer. Before climbing in, she glanced back at the criminal she knew so little about. His metallic chains slapped the sides of his bed aggressively as he continued to fight his memories. His torment, however, wasn't the only reason she looked back. She had been put on this ship for a specific reason and was paid a large sum of money to do something she hoped she wouldn't regret.

…

CHAPTER 18

Mission commander Charlie Miller spent most of the flight going over the maps and tactical mission graphics of their upcoming assault. Despite his experience, he couldn't help but feel the butterflies building in his stomach. The two hour five minute flight from their forward staged location at Scott Air Force Base in Illinois to Little Rock Air Force Base in Arkansas seemed to literally fly by.

The door gunner on the CH-47 Chinook looked at Major Charlie Miller and held up five fingers on his left hand. Five minutes. The gunner shouted it as well, but nobody could hear him over the powerful battering of rotors that propelled them through the dark night sky. Seeing the hand signal, the platoon of thirty that Charlie flew with each tapped his neighbor, and the same five minute sign was shown all the way down the line.

Upon the five minute notification, previously sleeping soldiers began sitting up in their black mesh seats, adjusting their rifles, and lowering the night vision goggles from their helmets to their eyes. Charlie put his map away and lowered his goggles as well. His goggles hummed as the batteries engaged the thermal and infrared electronics and a green light engulfed his right eye. At the same time, a third door gunner walked toward the end of the aircraft, lowered the ramp, and strapped himself into the rear M240 machine gun mounted on the back ramp. Whispering something into his microphone, the four helicopters dropped to exactly 100 feet above the ground to ensure they were below the radar capabilities of the target air force base.

Charlie recited the plan in his head. The first helicopter, consisting of his second platoon, would infiltrate the base and establish the outer perimeter and two support-by-fire positions in order to isolate the hangar from the security forces personnel. At the same time, the second helicopter would land on the far side of the airfield near the control tower. First platoon would seize the control tower and disable the communications platform. The assault force, his third platoon and the one he rode with, would land exactly two minutes after the first two helicopters touched down and assault the aircraft hangar. They would place timed charges on every jet and bomber they could find within five minutes. Exactly ten minutes after his company of Rangers landed on their airfield, they would egress the objective back to their CH-

47s and return to Scott Air Force base in Illinois. The fourth helicopter was his last platoon, which he opted to keep in reserve… just in case.

The gunner looked at him and signaled two minutes to touchdown by raising two fingers on his left hand. Already through his radio he could hear reports coming up from his first and second platoons. Charlie closed his eyes and prayed quietly one last time. While he typically prayed for safety, he refused to ask for that this time; instead he asked for peace. Charlie Miller would soon be the first Army officer in over two hundred and fifty years to attack his own countrymen on American soil. Charlie Miller and his company of Rangers were the catalyst for the next American Civil War.

CHAPTER 19

Despite the almost constant political rallies, interviews, and dinners, sleep continued to evade Evie Shepherd. With the clock half past two, she lay alone in her bed for two. Evie's eyes were heavy but not tired. Her mind bounced back and forth between the different events like a whack-a-mole club at a carnival. As soon as she had thought to death her latest speech, she found herself resurrecting a different part of the day, or week, or month. Regardless of the event, there was a common thread that wove through every purpose of her being. Jonah. Every talking event, every dinner, every charity, everything; all of it was for, and about, Jonah. And she *had* made progress. People were listening to her. They had heard and felt her plight. But most of all, she incited them to action. The people of the Free States believed her when she told them that the same events that plagued her could just as easily happen to them.

Jonah. The thought of his name sent tingles down her spine and into her toes. She pulled her cell phone off the night stand, twisted her pillow sideways to get a better angle, and started thumbing through old photos. She paused on a photo that showed them leaning together against an iron rail over-looking the beautiful Chesapeake Bay. Jonah wore a black suit with a cream dress shirt and a blue tie. Evie had never been quite sure the outfit matched, but Jonah never cared. She giggled out loud, remembering that night.

The photo was taken right before Jonah dropped the bracelet he had gotten her for their seventh anniversary into the ankle high water below. Jonah's expression was priceless when he realized what he did. His eyes got so big, and then a smile formed across his face. Jonah took off his shoes, climbed over the railing and lowered himself off the ledge. Using his cell phone as a flashlight, he searched for the bracelet between screams about rocks poking his feet and crabs gunning for his toes. Evie had laughed so hard that night, and when he finally emerged with the bracelet, his suit was soaked. But he had emerged victoriously and all future stories were of his heroism rather than his clumsiness. Evie smiled again in the empty bedroom and sighed. She really missed him.

Interrupting her thoughts, Evie felt the vibrations of her cell phone in her hand and watched as the display shifted from the photos to reveal an incoming call. *At two a.m.?* It was Governor John

Wilkes.

"How did you know I'd be awake?" she joked sarcastically.

"Didn't." his voice was raspy as if he'd just been woken up himself. "I just sent a car for you; we've got a crisis we have to deal with."

It wasn't like John to call her at odd hours. In fact, she couldn't remember a single time he had asked her to do anything after hours or while she was at home with her kids. "What about the kids?" she asked. "I can't just leave them."

"Don't worry, Susan's in the car and will help watch them."

"Susan?"

"My secretary, Evie… remember?"

"Ohh, right." She exclaimed, suddenly hoping the poor woman didn't over hear. "I'll be waiting downstairs; just don't have them ring the doorbell."

After thanking her for being so flexible, John hung up and Evie got dressed. She was happy to have a distraction. In the past two months, Evie finally understood Jonah's torment all too well: being left alone with her thoughts night after night while searching for sleep was a wretched way to spend an evening.

CHAPTER 20

As the black four door luxury town car rolled to a stop in front of the Governor's mansion, Evie could see John pacing back and forth impatiently on his porch. Seeing the car, he walked briskly towards it, opened the door before she could release the hatch herself and gave her a big but worried smile.

"Thank you so much for coming, Evie." He said graciously, placing a hand on her back shoulder and leading her up the circular red brick walkway towards the front door.

It was a pleasant night for May in Central Virginia. A gentle breeze swept through the four large white columns that boxed in the stairwell to the front door and rattled a wind chime from side to side. Through one of the downstairs windows encased in black shutters,

Evie could see a faint light emanating from the backroom.

"Are there others here, tonight?" Evie asked, suddenly realizing this may be bigger than just public relations.

"Yes; everyone who could make it in time came. Others will be here around noon." He stopped before they reached the door at the top of the brick steps and put his hand on Evie's shoulder, turning her towards him. "Evie, I sincerely appreciate everything that you've done for our cause so far." He sounded genuine but deeply distraught. "My intent was never to get you involved in a war though, Evie. Never."

"War?" She asked, stunned. "What do you mean? So quickly? There was rhetoric, but that was it!"

John looked around nervously, first at the street and then up towards the sky. "Let's talk more inside… these trees have ears."

Evie had been inside the Governor's mansion before, but in the dim three a.m. light, it looked mystical. The rustic pine floors radiated homey warmth that made you want to stay there for hours. Delicate crystal chandeliers hung from ornate coffered ceilings; but most of the lights were off.

The governor led Evie towards the back room; one she had seen but never entered. As she walked in, three men and a woman, engaged in intense conversation, stood up to greet her. John cleared his mouth to get the group's attention, wearily working a smile over his weathered face, "This is Evie Shepherd. She's been a wonderful asset to the team so far."

The four came over to introduce themselves. David Moore,

congressional delegate from 1ˢᵗ District in Virginia greeted her warmly. "Evie, such a wonderful opportunity to meet you. I just wish we could meet under better circumstances.

The second, Elizabeth Harris, an older lady who introduced herself as a delegate from Tennessee, welcomed her with eyes that were far wearier than the last; and with a face that was deeply apologetic. "Evie, I'm so sorry for your plight. Please know that my husband and I constantly pray for you and Jonah." Evie thanked her sincerely but was slowly becoming more alarmed with each passing moment. *What is going on?* She glanced to John beside her. Despite his sad and overwhelmed demeanor, he beamed with the pride of a father showing off his daughter to his friends.

The last two men came up together, and although they were dressed in jeans and t-shirts, she knew instantly they were military. Despite coming to the governor's house, the de facto leader of the separatist effort, they had dressed down. With as much military courtesy as existed, there was never any expectation that soldiers would dress up for an early morning impromptu visit… even if it was with the potential future president of the Free States. The older of the two men shook her hand and held it. "Paul Wilson. I worked with your husband many times, Evie." He had a deep steady voice, and his hands were warm. "This is my aid, Danny Young. Your husband was a great man. We worked together often, and I was deeply saddened to hear the news. If there is anything at all my family can do for you during this extremely difficult time, please, don't hesitate to ask."

"You're a general?" Evie asked, aware that if he had an aide- an aide willing to wake up at 2 a.m. - then he must be important.

"I suppose I am." He responded, smiling at her. Evie was overwhelmed with the open kindness these strangers showed her, but she couldn't escape the dread that rested deep in her gut. The kind of dread she imagined boxers felt before they got into the ring with each other. The kind of dread that only subsided after your opponent landed his first hit. Something was wrong; very wrong. With the introductions over, they took their seats.

Settling into his chair, John dove into the reason for their meeting. "At exactly 1205 this morning, a company of Rangers attacked Little Rock Air Force Base in Arkansas." Evie put her hand to her mouth, shocked. Looking around the room she realized she was the only one. Everyone else must have already known. "The Rangers destroyed a few cargo aircraft, disabled our communications tower, and killed 15 Security Forces personnel before escaping on helicopters."

Evie couldn't believe it. The war had really begun. "But why just that base? And why so limited?"

John turned towards Paul Wilson. "I think you have a better answer Paul."

"We don't think they intended for us to find out," the General started. "This was a limited incursion with very specific objectives. Little Rock is home to a portion of our strategic bomber fleet and the nearest base to the border with states aligned with the federalists." Paul paused to make sure she was still with him, and then glanced around the room. After receiving a nod from John, he continued. "We know they were after our bombers because we captured one of the soldiers."

Evie gasped. "You have a prisoner?"

"Yes, and so far he's being pretty cooperative. We know for certain they were after the bomber fleet, but the Rangers were dropped off at the wrong set of hangers. We think once they realized they were staring at cargo planes instead of bombers, they tried to make the movement by foot. Our security forces arrived in the middle of their movement and cut them off. Outnumbered, the platoon retreated to a position inside the hangar, and waited for their aircraft to pick them up."

"So what are you going to do?" Evie asked. She thought she knew the answer, but national politics wasn't anything she even pretended to understand. The answer was far simpler than she expected.

"We go to war, Evie," the governor said solemnly.

War. The three letter word that had been mentioned plenty of times, but never believed. It was a word that tore through her heart like a poisonous spear thrust by some ancient Persian warrior. She had sent her husband off to war too many times; had felt the sting of separation and the pain of loss. She had hovered near the phone at night hoping to get a phone call from the man she missed so much, and spent countless nights laying awake thinking about him. And now, war was rearing its ugly face again. "Why did you bring me here tonight? I'm no strategist. What use could I possibly be when discussing the brink of war?" Her mouth felt as dry as cotton.

"Evie, the people trust you. You aren't a politician or a military mind: we didn't bring you on board to be one. We brought you here because you have a story. Because you can identify with people that we can't, and because winning this war might mean bringing your husband out of exile. Do you understand what I'm saying Evie?"

Evie nodded. She did understand, and she found that deep down, she was still completely committed to their effort. "I do."

"Good. I've called an emergency meeting at four p.m. today to vote on a referendum authorizing war. I'd like you to be there… you don't have to speak, but just sitting by my wife's side says more about how we care for the families of our soldiers than anything else."

With the meeting over, John suggested she get some sleep before the emergency session, and offered her a car to return home. She gratefully accepted and took one last look around the historic home to take in the architecture, the smell of the wood, and the dimly lit chandeliers that saturated the walls and furniture with a warm autumn glow. Evie suspected that history was being made here tonight, and that years from now, when she sat with Jonah and reflected on all that it took for them to reunite, the secret conversations held here in this home, conversations that led the nation towards civil war, would play a pivotal role.

CHAPTER 21

Disaster. That was the only word that could summarize the events over the last four hours. A column of soldiers walked silently off the helicopter and toward the small debriefing room to the left of the landing pad. One hundred and thirty-one soldiers had boarded these Chinooks at 10:05 PM. One hundred and thirty returned; several of them wounded, one missing. *Disaster.*

While the men in his company went to the left to begin the debrief, Charlie Miller went right, walked past his soldiers receiving medical treatment without checking to see if they were okay, past the door to the operations center, and vomited in a small patch of grass on the far corner of the runway. Charlie felt it splatter, looked down at his boots and muttered a curse. He scuffed his tan boots across a clean part of the grassy corner and turned around to go back to the command building. After everything that happened, he supposed he was ready to face his commander who was sure to be irate.

The operations center was buzzing with activity. Charlie threw his bag in the corner, tore off his kit and headed to the back of the room to find his Commander, Colonel Rob Thorne. *Well, he doesn't look happy*, Charlie thought, spying him through the glass partition that separated his office from the operations floor.

"What the hell happened Charlie!?" he asked, when their eyes finally met.

"They dropped us off at the wrong damned hangar, and they knew we were coming!" Charlie aggressively responded; locking eyes with his boss to make sure Colonel Thorne knew how angry he was about the situation. They had worked together for a long time and he had a great relationship with him, but to come back from a secret mission with one soldier missing, three soldiers injured, and zero bombers destroyed, was bad news.

Colonel Thorne didn't respond. He was gazing past him now at the large screen in the front of the room. Charlie turned around to see their unmanned aerial vehicle following a convoy of police cars with an ambulance in the center. "Is that him?" Charlie asked.

"We think so."

"Where is he?"

"Texas."

"Texas, in two hours!? How did they get him there so fast?!"

"They put him on an aircraft as soon as your team left… they must have known we'd try to get him back."

"And we will, right?" Charlie insisted, leaning in towards his boss intently.

"That's not our call anymore, Charlie."

Charlie didn't say anything, but continued watching the feed on the TV. The police cars on the black and white screen took an exit at the highway and turned left on the side streets. Suddenly, Charlie recognized where they were. "They're taking him to Fort Hood, aren't they?"

"That's what we think." As Colonel Thorne spoke those four words, the feed on their drone went dead. Someone was either blocking their feed, or had shot down the aircraft. Either way, it didn't matter, the fate of his soldier was officially out of his hands. This was a night that Charlie Wilson would forever remember. The second War Between the States had begun – and it started in a way none of them had ever planned.

CHAPTER 22

Logan Carter thoroughly enjoyed his job. While not many people could do what he did, seven days a week, twelve hours a day, Logan found it altogether pleasant and relaxing. He didn't mean to say that other people physically couldn't do what he did. After all, it was really just sitting behind a computer screen eating chips – Cheetos being his favorite. What he meant was, there were very few people that *would* actually want to do what he did. After all, sitting in isolation for twelve hours a day waiting for the one chance to turn a key and push a button didn't seem like much fun to most people. Especially when that one chance was really an opportunity that had never happened; and when, if it did happen, you would be the sole survivor responsible for initiating nuclear war. For all of those reasons Logan believed it wasn't a popular job by many standards; but for those reasons, especially the isolation, he was grateful to have this as his.

The soft glow of his computer screen bounced gently off Logan's face and reflected off the lenses of his glasses. In the reflection, a visitor would be able to see he wasn't researching new types of nuclear warheads or standing ready to receive some special eight character code that would initiate a world-ending sequence. Instead, as he did every other night for a few hours before opening a book, Logan played solitaire.

Nestled deep in the North Dakota countryside, Minot Air Force Base was really the perfect place for Logan. The winters were tough, but he had grown up in the North Country his whole life. He moved his first king, the king of spades, to an empty spot and slapped a queen on top. He loved making progress, but the best reward was watching cards cascade across the screen. The clock on the wall ticked to half past two. He was six hours away from another successful shift. Logan came to define success when three things occurred. First, he had to win at least three games of solitaire in a row. He came to do this easily now. Second, he expected to read at least four chapters of his latest novel. Lastly, and some would argue most importantly, he wanted to not be the person that ended the world with the push of a button. If he could do those three things with minimal distraction, he would go home happy, wipe the Cheetos dust off his fingers, climb into the shower and then the bed, and wake up in time for the next shift. Logan found his second ace, the ace of hearts and double-clicked to put it on the top. Having already found the two of hearts, Logan was pleased to see his computer automatically move it to the top as well; exposing the coveted nine he was waiting for.

Subtle vibrations from helicopter rotors were not uncommon near Minot AFB, even at two am. And as Logan moved card after card, inching ever closer to victory, he could feel the deep drone of helicopter blades. But then, something wholly unexpected happened; something he had never seen in his twelve years working here. Everything went black.

"What the hell," Logan muttered under his breath, searching for his cell phone to provide enough light to reach his land line. Finally finding it and depressing the button, Logan found himself disappointed a second time when his phone failed to turn on. "What the hell," he muttered again, continuing to fumble for his land line in the dark. In his bunker, deep under the ground, it wasn't just dark, it was pitch black. The windowless bunker was so dark Logan couldn't see his hand in front of his face. Finally, finding the phone and raising it to his head, Logan was dumbfounded, the line was completely dead. "What the hell," he said, a bit louder and with frustration boiling up into his voice.

Logan stumbled his way through the dark, bumped his shin into a stool, knocked a paper off the table, and went in the direction of the large steel door that sealed him into his portion of the bunker. Logan had always found it a bit humorous that after twelve years of working in the same office, he still couldn't remember much about the layout. He guessed he just hadn't paid much attention to some of the specifics. Regardless, reaching what he suspected was the door, he felt for the swipe pad, found it, and rubbed his card against the device and waited expectantly for it to initiate a lever that would open the heavy steel blast door. The door did nothing. The pad made no noise, no levers were engaged, and the door did not open.

Logan turned around in the dark bunker and sat down with his back to the wall. *This cannot be happening. Locked in? How does that happen? How on earth does a state of the art facility lose all power?* Then the dreaded answer rushed into his mind, causing his hair to prickle up the back of his neck. *Are we under attack?* As if on cue, a heavy crack smashed into the other side of the steel door followed by three more cracks of equal ferocity. *Gunfire.* Logan sprung away from the door, stumbled over the stool that he had moved out of his way mere minutes before, fell on his belly, and crawled under his desk. He could hear noises now on the outside, as if someone was fiddling with the secure entrance into his space.

Logan couldn't be sure what happened next, but the intense pressure that followed left him struggling to maintain consciousness. Whatever occurred, it had pushed him from the cover of his desk to the far end of the room. With his ears ringing, his eyes strained to see in the blackness through blurry, tear-filled vision. Blinking repeatedly, Logan thought he could see the faintest green dot of light hover above him. He tried desperately to move his head, but couldn't. His toes tingled and hands still vibrated.

"What's going on?" he said through slurred speech, still blinking, trying to make sense of the green light.

A flashlight turned on from his left but he couldn't turn his head to see. Hands came down across his neck and removed the key card he kept beneath his shirt. "We're going to borrow this," a thick accent whispered into his ear.

CHAPTER 23

His eyes strained to focus. Everything was blurry. He closed them again. *Had it been five months?* Whatever gas had been flowing through the mask was now shut off. He was relieved. He had just spent the last five months reliving some of the worst moments of his career over, and over, and over again.

A hand touched his shoulder, and a familiar voice spoke. "Sir, I'm going to remove your mask now. In a few minutes I'll move you to the vessel taking you down to the surface."

Jonah opened his eyes again and tried to concentrate. The ship was dark except for a dim row of lights lining the aisle. He could see a shadow moving to his right. The young girl and her family were also awake. *So we've made it to Mars,* Jonah thought. He truly did not believe this day would come. It was hard to admit, but several times he found himself wishing the ship would crash and he wouldn't have to face what would surely come next. Dread coated his insides and gurgled up into his throat. His heart ached and his stomach was nauseous. *Mars.*

Across the aisle he could see the stewardess helping the family undo their lap and shoulder harnesses. "This way, honey," she said, as she led the girl to the hatch on the floor in the center of the ship. The hatch opened and a thin step-ladder extended below to their landing vessel. After some time, she came back for each parent. Jonah still had trouble focusing. She must have woken him up last.

Finally, she came for him. "Sir, I'm going to unlock your shackles from the seat and stand you up. I want to remind you that the chains around your wrists contain an electrical impulse. Should you try to escape, I will initiate the pulse to paralyze you."

Jonah nodded and the stewardess unlocked his harness and disconnected his shackles from the seat. She helped him stand but his legs were wobbly. "Careful," she said. "You haven't used those in a few months."

Weak-kneed and staggering, he was led to the hatch and then down the narrow stairs and into the vessel. The smaller ship was an oval shape and looked more like a submarine than a spacecraft. There were ten seats lining the walls and facing inward. The family looked stunned to see him again.

"Miss! Why are you loading him into the same pod? We aren't

going to the same place." Steve complained, disturbed that Jonah continued to keep them company.

She smiled. "They will separate you when you land. These pods are expensive, you know."

Steve scowled.

Jonah looked at Zoe. "Don't worry, I won't hurt you." As soon as he uttered the words, Steve's head snapped up. Regretting saying anything, Jonah imagined the effects of the gas had left him feeling brave.

"Don't speak to her," Steve hissed.

Jonah looked at him for a moment and then at the ground. *Just a criminal*, he thought.

As the stewardess completed her final checks, she took one last look at Jonah, reached up to a hook above the hatch, and hung the key to an eye shaped bolt above his chains.

"Good luck," she said, then leaned in and whispered into his ear. "Contact Icarus on satellite channel 32... we will remain in orbit." Then, she stepped out and sealed the hatch. Jonah's head spun. *Was she one of theirs? Did she belong to the rebellion? What did she mean? Why couldn't she have said more?* Steve looked up at the key, then at Jonah, and finally at Amy. It seemed he couldn't believe that the stewardess would be so stupid as to put the key to a convict's chains in the same craft! He started to stutter something but then stopped. He must have finally believed his protests were of no use.

Gas from the seal hissed as the capsule pressurized. The craft jerked gently as the pod disengaged from the transport ship. After several seconds of floating away from the spaceship, the landing pod's engines whined and fired a single pulse to project them towards the planet below. Steve looked at Amy and Zoe, and smiled. Soon the small capsule was hurtling towards Mars. The small circular windows were black but soon lit up with red and white light as they entered the atmosphere. The ship vibrated violently. Zoe gripped her armrests. Steve leaned his head back against his seat and closed his eyes. Jonah's chains clanked back and forth as they descended deep into the Martian atmosphere.

Down they hurtled, farther and farther into Mars, and farther from Evie and his kids. Then, at last, they were through the atmosphere and into the thin air that was characteristic of the Martian troposphere. Chained to his seat, Jonah was blind to his surroundings; thankfully an excited Zoe started calling out features of the surface.

"Look at that crater…"

"… and those mountains!"

"…where's all the water?"

Jonah did his best to hide a smile. Her joy was refreshing. He had been burdened far too long and this tiny reprieve warmed his heart, if only for a moment. Zoe had straight black hair, and freckles sprinkled across her face. She gave off an air that screamed carefree exuberance. Jonah suddenly felt as if he'd been punched in the gut. Zoe reminded him so much of the teenager he pictured Eden becoming. Jonah thought back to Eden. He thought about her teenage years and how beautiful she would be.

How all the boys would try to talk to her and come by the house. How he'd have to fight them off and strike fear in their hearts. About how he couldn't… because he was here… about how he intended to do whatever he needed to, so that he could get back to them.

The craft jerked as its parachute deployed, jolting Jonah out of his reverie. Down they floated, closer and closer to the surface. And then, the windows went black and the craft fell through the sun baked crust and into a carved out loading area deep within the Martian surface. Finally, the pod touched down and anchors that looked like robotic legs deployed from the sides to keep it upright. The parachute draped gently over the craft as the massive hangar doors sealed them off from the atmosphere above.

Patiently, the family waited. They waited for someone to get them off the ship and away from the criminal. Jonah, on the other hand, was more than happy to wait forever, and that is exactly what happened. They just waited.

****

Jane watched from the ship until the craft had descended through the atmosphere. Her chief responsibility was to ensure that their ship did not leave orbit. She returned to her chair and entered a code into the arm rest causing a small storage container to open. While virtually no one was willing to bring a firearm onboard a ship because of the associated risks of a bullet piercing the ship's hull, stun guns were sufficient, both because they did not contain the materiel that would set off metal detectors and because they were still more than capable of achieving the desired objectives. This particular gun contained enough voltage to drop an elephant in a matter of seconds and would adequately boil the blood inside the pilots before they were able make sense of what was happening.

Jane held the stun gun tightly against her black and green Unicore jumpsuit and walked quickly towards the cockpit. As she ascended the dimly lit steps towards the front of the ship, she could hear the two telling bad space jokes. They heard her approach and the copilot turned around.

"Hey Jane, how do astronauts serve dinner?"

Jane smiled, raised the gun from her right hand to within a few feet of the man's head, and squeezed the trigger. His expression changed from the dumb smile to a flat stare moments before the voltage slammed him in the skull like a jack hammer breaking up concrete. The pilot had turned to watch but clearly was having trouble processing what had just happened. Jane twisted her body in the small cabin to achieve the most accurate shot and squeezed the trigger a second time. Before he had a chance to stand to his feet, the electricity from the stun gun had raced through his body and stopped his heart. He clenched his teeth, gripped his hands into fists and fell from his chair.

Jane stepped passed his lifeless body, leaned over the sleek silver keyboard, and typed a command into the computer ensuring they would remain in orbit. Moving to the communications panel, she switched the channel on their satellite receiver from 13 to 32, and went to wake up Icarus, the man who had boarded their ship at the moon. As she strode gracefully to the back of the ship, she had to admit she felt good. Five months was a long time in between jobs. If she was going to be honest with herself, Jane would have to admit that she had been terrified something was going to go wrong.

CHAPTER 24

Malek ran his tongue across his short pointy teeth. Since the rebellion, there were two camps that vied for power on Mars. Whenever his army got the chance to capture someone from the other camp they did so with zeal and gusto. The men would toy with the prisoner until they grew tired. These were, after all, convicts. But you had to be smart; so Malek also made sure they exploited the prisoner for information, and then, once all their desires had been fulfilled, they would execute their captive. Whenever his men got the opportunity to capture someone young and 'untainted', so to speak, however, they brought her to Malek as a gift. A tribute, if you will, to declare their unending loyalty towards Malek, their king.

The table was set with crudely crafted plates and bowls, knives and forks. Cups were made from the copper that miners drew from deep within the Mars. Inside the bowls was the most extravagant display of fruits and vegetables available on Mars, courtesy of the subterranean farms worked deep beneath the surface.

Early achievements in genetically modified crops were nothing compared to what they were now experiencing on Mars. Thanks to the research of the pioneers of the Martian expeditions, the plants were capable of growing in extremely austere conditions. While Malek didn't know every detail, he remembered enough billboards and news clips showing their early progress, first in lava fields on Earth, and after they were perfected, in the Martian underground.

His eight generals sat around his table, while he held the seat of honor at the head. These were the eight most loyal men in his small army, and the ones Malek could count on to give their all for his cause. Their tradition was to feast together twice a year – to dine on the tribute his men brought him from the miner's camp, something any king could truly appreciate.

This time their gift looked delectable. In the center of the table was a beautiful young girl, not older than fifteen or sixteen and barely clothed. She was strapped to the wooden table. The girl shivered from the cold and trembled out of fear of what they were preparing to do to her. Tears ran down her cheeks and she quietly whimpered. Her dark brown hair had been fanned out by Malek's cooks and rested delicately across the top of the table to act as a placemat for the king's plate. They had caught her in the farms below, a deserter from the miner's camp.

While the farms provided all the sustenance his small army needed, they always found that they missed the taste of the meat they'd eaten on Earth. Cattle simply weren't sustainable and chickens had to be fed and nourished only to provide so little food. People though – especially the miners – were in abundance. The hard work had stripped away the fat from their bones, leaving behind nothing but the protein, something they found themselves constantly craving. While one chicken barely fed one of his soldiers, a miner fed his whole council. So why should he not delight? After all – he was Malek. Their King. Their god. And his men desired desperately to please him.

Malek licked his lips again, eager to partake in the feast prepared specially for him. In the dimly lit dining room, shadows crept across his face as he rose. His men could see the sores on his face caused by exposure to the Martian atmosphere during the rebellion. Radiation had scorched his neck staining it dark red. His hands were discolored and charred.

Malek's lips curled upward, showing a row of filed front teeth. Just as he prepared to address them, one of his guards ran in. "Malek! A ship, a ship came into the hanger!" he wheezed.

His generals all pushed their chairs out and left the room. Malek sighed and leaned in towards the girls face. Sticking out his tongue, he licked from the corner of her mouth upwards towards her ear; and then whispered. "I guess we'll have to eat you later." Malek left the room and the girl let out an exhausted cry of relief mixed with fear.

CHAPTER 25

After some time looking out the small port window into the massive hangar, Steve decided he had waited long enough. "Let's go, Amy. If they aren't going to welcome us, we'll find them."

Jonah spoke up. "Something's not right. There's nothing going on out there. You shouldn't leave the ship until someone comes to get you."

"What do you know, criminal?" Steve snorted. "Get unbuckled, Amy. Help Zoe out too."

"Steve, maybe he's right… this is weird…" Amy replied, not sure why she would support the man in chains over her husband. Looking out the window, all she saw was trash and part of the orange parachute that had slowed their decent through the atmosphere that now rested gently alongside the craft. There was nothing else. It was completely and utterly deserted.

"Steve." Jonah said, almost pleading with him. "Come on, Steve. Look out there. There's nobody around. Stay here with your family. Get that key down, unlock me, and I'll make sure it's safe."

Steve roared with laughter. "You don't really think I'd unlock you, do you? How stupid do you think I am?" He looked at Amy, "They don't send thieves to Mars Amy, and I'm not interested in this creep eying our daughter any longer. Let's go."

As they stood up, they staggered a bit. Having not used their legs in months, they looked like newborn fawns walking for the first time. After some difficulty, the family climbed through a small doorway and exited down the ladder and off the ship. Walking away, Steve was clearly still surprised. Looking for affirmation, he turned to Amy. "Can you believe that guy? He actually thought I was stupid enough to set him free!"

Amy changed the subject. "Where is everybody, Steve?"

The hanger the silver pod had landed in was massive. It had been carved into the thick iron and granite rock that blanketed the Martian landscape. The floor was a slick metallic substance and reflected their images almost as good as a mirror would. Steve stared at the floor for a moment before moving forward. It wasn't polished as if it had been maintained, but it was very reflective. He scuffed it with his foot but left no marks. *The future of landing pads*, he thought. There were two tunnels that exited the hanger – each looked identical and were offset at a 45 degree angle from one another.

For no reason in particular, Steve chose the tunnel on the right.

"They're probably right around the corner, Amy. Relax, look at us! We made it to Mars!"

She smiled. He was right. They had finally made it to their new home and all that was left would be to settle in and make friends. They could finally start over.

Just then they heard clanging down the hallway as the shadows of four figures appeared.

"Finally," muttered Steve. He waved his arms above his head and shouted to them. "Hey, over here! Took you guys long enough!"

The figures didn't respond audibly, but started moving faster towards them until finally they were jogging.

"What on earth are they doing?" Steve said to Amy.

For a moment the three just stood there, watching the four figures come towards them when suddenly it dawned on Steve that the criminal was right. Something was off here. Seriously off.

Is that a club he's carrying? "Run!" Steve shouted. The three turned but it was too late. Amy's legs moved with all the sluggishness that was expected from spending months in a partial stasis and slipped on the slick hanger floor. Steve turned to help her up but the four were already on them. The man in the front swung the club above his head and struck Steve hard across the jaw.

****

Whipping her head around to the sound of something breaking, Zoe looked back just long enough to see her father hit the ground. Blood sprayed across the wall. Her mother screamed for help as the other three descended on them both. Zoe didn't look back again but became acutely aware that the screaming had stopped. She ran as fast as she could back to the only place she could think of; back to the ship, back to the prisoner, and hopefully, back to safety.

Climbing up the ladder and into the pod she screamed. "Help me, help me; please help me!"

"The key, get the key!" shouted Jonah.

Zoe was a mess. Sobbing, she fumbled for the key. Missing it once. Twice. Finally, she grabbed it and pulled it off the hook.

"Get me out of these chains!" Jonah insisted. He didn't want to stress her out even more, but judging by the shaking and crying he knew it was bad. He knew someone was coming.

A shadow. Two shadows. Voices. "Hurry, Zoe!"

Her hands were shaking as she fit the key into the lock. He could see hands gripping the bars, followed by a face as it pulled itself up the steep stairs. The face was covered in sores. His hair was patchy, growing out in globs on his disheveled head. In his hand was a wooden club. At first it didn't look like he saw Jonah or Zoe as he was coming up the stairs. He approached slowly, scanning the pod until their eyes met.

Frantically, Zoe fumbled the lock. "Zoe!" Jonah shouted, and at last the lock broke free.

The disheveled human being sprinted up the last few rungs and charged at Jonah through the small doorway that separated the ladder from the crew compartment of the pod. As he approached, he raised the club above his head to strike Jonah, who was still trying to get out of his seat. Chains connected to his wrists, Jonah finally leapt to his feet. The club came down, but Jonah stepped wide to his right, taking advantage of the man's expectation that he was still chained in place. The club missed. Jonah front-kicked him in the gut, sending him flying backwards against the far wall of the ship. The metal clanged and the man grunted, collapsing to his knees. Jonah clenched his hands together and raised them above the disheveled man's head — bringing them down over the base of his spine. With a loud pop, the man collapsed to the ground.

Turning back to the stairs he could hear more clamoring. Jonah grabbed the bat and threw it as soon as he saw the man's torso. Impact. Another grunt. The sound of someone falling down the stairs. *Time to go on the offensive.* "Stay here!" Jonah shouted at Zoe, racing down the ladder before the second attacker could get to his feet. Climbing on top of him, he wrapped his chains around the man's neck and pulled. His muscles strained from months of not being used, but they strengthened quickly as blood rushed back into them.

The wiry haired man flailed, he clawed with his filthy grown out finger nails and grunted. Then, nothing. Even though his body fell limp, Jonah kept the chains around his neck until he was certain there was no life left in him. The man's eyes glazed over as he passed from this world to the next, and the look in his eyes reflected only a lifeless shell that previously housed a soul. Instantly, Jonah left the present and was pulled back to his wars, back to the girl in the canal, and back to the men that he had lost.

Trapped and tormented, Jonah couldn't escape his thoughts until Zoe pulled him out of them with a distant scream which snapped him out of his trance. Looking around, he saw two more in the tunnel charging him; a bald man and his emaciated counterpart. He searched for the bat and found it behind one of the feet from the landing pod. Loosening the chains off his wrists, he gripped the end of the chains in his right hand and the bat in his left.

The two were smaller than the first, but they weren't taken by surprise like the others were. As they approached, one moved off to his left, the other to his right. Now the tactics began. Jonah circled counter-clockwise and backwards throughout the large hangar, always keeping them from getting behind him.

The man to his right with the bald head stepped in. Jonah slapped the chain towards his face causing the man to retreat out of range.

Continuing to circle each other, the bald man spoke. "Put down that club man, we ain't gonna hurt you."

"Who are you?" Jonah demanded, still circling.

"Judging by your clothes, we're just like you man. Congratulations… you just earned your freedom."

These were the prisoners. This couldn't be. Had they escaped? Were they in control? Sure, he was free… but at the cost of the brutality he had just witnessed?

Jonah was not interested. With Zoe in the ship, there was no way he would put his club down and abandon her. Only the Lord knew what they might do to young Zoe if he surrendered.

"Put your clubs down first. Then, maybe, we'll talk." Jonah finally replied.

"Dude, this guy's something else," the gaunt-looking one said to his fat, bald accomplice. "Kill him."

Years of military conflict and experience gave Jonah the advantage, and he was prepared for what came next. Before the words "kill" could exit the convict's mouth, Jonah leapt towards the balding man with blinding speed. The convict, who had just glanced at his talking partner, was caught entirely off guard. Jonah whipped the chain towards his face. Instinctively, the man raised his club in defense. *Predictable.* At the same time, Jonah brought his own club down hard on the convicts arm. He heard a snap and the barbed-wire club fell flatly to the ground.

Now, inside the convict's grip, Jonah grabbed the grimacing man by the collar and spun him around towards his friend. Human shield. He could see over the bald man's shoulder that the other convict was charging towards them. Jonah separated himself from the wounded convict and shoved him hard towards the oncoming assault. The thin man did his best to shrug off his chunkier partner but it was too late. Jonah was too strong and too fast. As soon as the man had escaped the body of his accomplice, Jonah brought his club down on his collar bone. The convict dropped to the ground. Once, twice, three times he hit him.

Having successfully subdued the immediate threat, he moved back to the bald convict, who was clutching his arm in pain and writhing on the floor. Deciding it was more civilized to strangle him than smash his face in, Jonah approached the man from behind and wrapped his chains around his neck; this time making sure not to look into the man's eyes as he did it.

With the fight over and sweating from exertion, Jonah searched their bodies but found nothing. Switching out his bare club for the barbed-wire one, he made his way back to the ship to find Zoe.

Zoe sat nervously in her seat. The tears had stopped, but her makeup was streaked down her cheeks; her hair was in disarray. To Jonah, she was still just a child. When she saw Jonah she seemed relieved at first, but it quickly faded and was replaced by shock and fear as she realized that she was staring at a convict that had been in chains mere minutes before. Had she been able to reconcile that with the fact that he had just smashed four men's skulls in, she probably would have screamed.

Jonah knelt down next to her. "I'm so sorry." He reached out towards her hand but she pulled away, and started crying again. She didn't trust him. He wasn't sure he would trust him either if he was her. Jonah let her cry for a few minutes while looking nervously out the window. In the tunnel he could see people moving the bodies of her mother and father.

"Zoe, it's not safe here. We have to go."

Zoe looked up at him, but didn't say anything,

Jonah continued. "Zoe, I know it's hard to trust me. I know the way I looked in those chains. I know what your father said. Please, believe me, I will never do anything to hurt you. But right now, whether you believe me or not, you need to listen to me. You need to get out of that seat, take my hand, and get off this ship; because if we don't leave in the next five minutes, we are going to be completely surrounded by whoever that was out there."

He held out his hand. "Come on, Zoe. We have to go."

Reluctantly, she took his hand and let him lead her off the ship. Jonah wished he didn't have to lead her past the four bodies, but he had no choice. Pools of blood had begun to run together on the floor, magnified by the mirror effect of the meticulous material that covered the ground. Next to him, he could hear Zoe gag. Jonah ignored it and tugged on her hand to move her faster down the opposite tunnel. *We've got to find somewhere to lay low*, Jonah thought.

CHAPTER 26

Malek was spitting mad. "What?!" he boomed when he found out that four of his guards had been killed at the hand of a single convict.

"…And you! You watched from the tunnel the whole time!?"

Malek sat high above the two in his throne chair carved from the same red stone they mined beneath the surface. He couldn't believe what he was hearing. Four of his warriors murdered, and the other two he had sent with the party retreated. Something would have to be done. The two stammered on, trying to explain what they had seen and why they didn't help, but Malek wasn't listening. He had heard enough.

Malek sighed and motioned for silence. Disgusted, he looked to the observers lining the walls of the long, rectangular room. "Let their example be a lesson to you. Because of the cowardice displayed by these pathetic men, they will be executed."

As the group cheered, the two cowards were led away.

"Find him and bring him to me!" Malek ordered his generals. Seething with anger, he looked toward the dining room. The girl was still on the table, pale and shivering. "Put her in the prison," he barked at others, "I'm not hungry anymore."

Malek followed the execution procession down the hallway. After a few hundred yards the hallway opened up into a second aircraft hangar. Three ships were parked close to one wall but the rest of the hanger was open. In the center, the convicts had placed two tables. Escorts on both sides of the now bound men lifted them onto the tables and sat them back to back. The men trembled. Above them hung a massive stone, elevated by a cable, and connected to a lever. It was a crude form of execution, but it sufficed. It also served as a valuable demonstration to those who would disobey him.

Malek stepped towards the center and addressed the two. "For your cowardice, you are being executed," Malek said plainly. Then, looking to the crowd, "I expect you to die for your brothers! Anyone that would prefer to come back to the safety of our camp after witnessing their brothers murdered is not worthy to live here!" He looked to the man at the lever on the far end of the hangar wall. "Release the stone."

The rest of the convicts cheered as the stone came crushing down, obliterating the men beneath it.

Unfazed, Malek walked through the crowd and back to his chair.

CHAPTER 27

Jonah and Zoe started out jogging but were now walking briskly through the maze of reddish tunnels underneath the Martian surface. Jonah could hear Zoe breathing heavily, trying to match his pace and stride. He didn't slow down. Jonah preferred to have Zoe focus on the physical activity of moving through the tunnels, rather than what just happened in the landing bay.

Finally, Zoe piped up. "I can't walk as fast as you," she panted.

"I'm sorry Zoe, but we have to keep moving." Jonah replied.

Zoe was serious, and after a few more moments she slowed down and then stopped completely, her features set in a stubborn line.

"I'm not going any farther. I can't." she protested.

Without taking his attention away from his surroundings, Jonah stopped walking and turned towards her. He didn't know what to say, but was sure she would break down if the weight of what had just happened had a chance to truly sink in.

Instead of collapsing under the weight of her circumstances, however, her eyes fixed on him accusingly. "Who are you?" she demanded. "I'm not going any farther with you. You're just a criminal. I saw what you did to those guys. Tell me who you are and why you were sent here."

Jonah sighed. This wasn't the conversation he wanted to have potentially moments away from being attacked by the gang of convicts. *How long had they been walking? 20 or 30 minutes? How much of a head start did they get?* Instead of answering, Jonah looked around again. A side channel, a cave, anything that they could hide in.

"I'm serious!" Zoe continued. "I'm not going to walk down this awful tunnel with a criminal unless you explain to me why you're here!"

"Zoe, I know you won't believe me, but I'm not a criminal…I'm innocent. Let's just leave it at that for now. I would never hurt you, ok?" Zoe stubbornly looked past him, refusing to make eye contact any longer. Look, we have to keep moving. We need to find a place to hide."

Jonah turned to start walking again but she didn't move.

"Who are you?" she demanded. "If you're innocent why are you here? I saw what you did to those guys back there; only criminals would kill that easily."

Struggling to maintain a balance between her need for information and his need to keep moving, he decided to explain as quickly as he could. "Zoe… I was a soldier. I was arrested and tried for conspiracy and treason." Jonah paused, and then continued. "I'm a father and a husband. I have three children. One of them is a little girl. I've never hurt anyone that wasn't an enemy," he implored. "Please trust me. We have to find a place to hide."

"And your name?"

Shaking his head but feeling more pity than irritation, he said "It's Jonah. My name is Jonah."

Zoe paused for a moment longer and then finally spoke again. "Fine, I'll go with you… but on one condition. Stop walking so fast. This sucks enough as it is."

Jonah faked a smile. "You set the pace, but we don't have much time."

Not before long, they came to another break in the tunnels – one went up, the other down. The route upwards was well lit. The route down and to the left was dark. Jonah chose to head down because his training demanded it. Whenever you were behind enemy lines and on the run, you found the nastiest place possible to hide, and this time, it would be easier to hide in the dark. Large bars blocked the path, but they were spaced out enough for Jonah and Zoe to slip through. As they walked in the darkness, the tunnel began to slope. Deeper and deeper they descended into the belly of Mars. The rocks glistened with moisture from the dim light coming from the entrance. At last, the hill seemed to level out and they were on flat ground. The tunnel floor had given way to dirt and soil. And then, finally, it opened up.

Beyond the entrance was a great expanse of underground farms. The genetically modified plants let off a gentle green glow reminiscent of a movie that combined *Children of the Corn* and *K-19* – a nuclear disaster onboard a Russian submarine. Jonah remembered the farm articles about early Martian settlements. The plants were fueled by organic substances already existing in the Martian soil. As part of a chemical reaction, they emitted a spectrum of light, some ultraviolet light that enabled the plants to get the remaining energy they needed from each other. The settlers then harvested the plants for food. But there was another important characteristic. All these tunnels had been sealed off from the surface. The plants generated oxygen and pumped it through the caverns. Scientists had actually created an ecosystem capable of supporting life.

The farms, although rich and plentiful, looked like they had been largely abandoned. Using the glow of the dim green light, Jonah circled the fields clockwise, searching for a dry spot to lie down and rest. Despite sleeping for almost five months he felt drained and exhausted. Finally, he spotted a cleft of rocks along the far wall. Jonah climbed up first, examined the space, and then pulled Zoe up. *This would do.* Zoe didn't say anything but curled up beside him. He could tell she was crying again. Not knowing how to comfort her, Jonah leaned back against the rough wall. Eventually, he fell asleep.

CHAPTER 28

The mornings were the toughest for Evie. After restless nights, she had to force herself to climb out of bed to get a head start before the children. The key to living with three children and no husband was a disciplined lifestyle and painstaking routine. The routine was both her worst enemy and her best friend, her discipline merely enforced it. Each morning she would creep out of bed, snag her robe off the door, and tip toe silently down the long hallway that connected her room to a small carpeted alcove containing a leather chair, a computer table, and a coffee maker.

While she loved the peace and quiet that the early morning afforded her, the silence also tormented her. It wasn't just the silence itself that caused her heart to ache, it was the desire for true companionship that only Jonah could offer. Evening and morning, Evie had only the kids to share and experience life with. When she laughed, it was with children over funny but childish things, and when she cried it was alone. Guarded from despair, Evie simply kept her routine. It was the thing that kept her occupied and, in a sense, kept her sane.

Every morning, she would wake at four a.m. and begin to write. Aside from her speaking engagements, John Wilkes had insisted that she provide the Richmond Times a daily opinion article that would be published with the morning paper. She always worked two days ahead to make sure she didn't have to rush her piece for the following day but that also allowed her to write about something current enough to matter. If she had written a week out, she would lose the public to other opinions, and if she wrote too soon, she might lack the research and editing that made her piece worth reading. The articles she wrote were almost a form of therapy for her. Sometimes when she typed, she would close her eyes and pretend to tell Jonah that she was avenging him. That she hadn't stopped working the entire time he slept on the spaceship that hurtled him away from her at ever increasing speeds. Now that she thought about it, the spaceship may finally be slowing down or could even already be at Mars!

She looked at her watch and counted back the months on her fingers. It was March and Jonah left in October. What little she knew about his journey could be summarized in that it would take about five months. If that was the case, then he might be waking from his stasis. She shuddered to think of him waking up in the cold darkness of space, hovering above the blood red planet he was to call home. Suddenly, the topic for her next article fluttered into her mind. Seated in a brown recliner with a laptop on her legs and a warm cup of creamy coffee on the table, she began to type. *Then and Now: The last five months that dictate the rest of our lives.* She didn't intend it to read like a eulogy or hopeless blabber, but each word she typed drove her into a deeper depression. Just as Evie thought she couldn't type any longer, her phone rang and caused their youngest to cry. Looking to see who it was, she kicked herself for not turning her phone on silent. It was John Wilkes.

CHAPTER 29

Jonah could hear the trees rustle. It was a hot day and the rustling sound of the soft sway of plants caught in a breeze was a welcome relief from the scorching sun. He slowly canted his face in the direction of the breeze, trying unsuccessfully to find relief from the heat. A bead of sweat dripped out of his helmet, down his nose, and plopped onto a blade of grass below. He looked to his left. The three were alert and looking down a dusty road. He scanned to his right to find the other side of his security effectively positioned in the other direction. A classic ambush. He didn't need to look back; he knew what would be there. About 100 meters to his rear was a maneuver force waiting for his signal. They had been lying in an orchard near a "T" intersection for nearly three days now; waiting for an insurgent army to leave the safety of its village.

"Jonah," someone whispered. He looked around. No one was

speaking. *The rustle of the trees grew louder and the breeze stronger, but he couldn't feel it.*

"Jonah," she whispered again, this time more violently. Someone was shaking him. It was Zoe. Groggily, Jonah opened his eyes and found himself as far away from the orchard as possible. A feeling of detached numbness washed over him as he realized he wasn't even on Earth. "Jonah," she whispered again, "something is moving the plants."

Zoe pointed to the center of the farm. Jonah strained in the dim green light to see where she was pointing. Sure enough, a wide swath of tall green crops was gently moving back and forth in the center of the field, but there was no wind this deep in the cave. There was no noise, no rustle of leaves, just the gentle back and forth sway of the corn. As the pale green plants swayed, their light cast faint shadows on the ceiling of the cave.

"Are those people back?" Zoe whispered. She gripped his forearm firmly as she spoke, fear radiating from her face.

"Stay low, Zoe," he whispered back. "I don't know." Jonah was shocked to even think that those convicts could have snuck up on them. *How could they possibly have gotten down here without me hearing? Why aren't they making any noise?* Something wasn't right. Not right at all. Jonah's hair prickled and a shiver crawled up his spine to the base of his neck. He knew whatever was in the field were not the convicts, but what it was, he didn't know and he certainly didn't want to find out. With his free hand, Jonah quietly searched for his club, partially hidden behind a rock. Squaring his shoulders, he prepared for the worst. They weren't coming off this cleft of rocks without a fight.

Zoe and Jonah watched the plants for what seemed like an eternity. How much time had passed was impossible to tell; once fear and adrenaline seized a person, time was a fleeting sense at the whims of its beholder. Eventually, the plants stopped moving. There was nothing; no noise, no movement, and no light other than the eerie green glow coming off the crops. They waited for a few moments longer in silence before Zoe broke the stillness with her young voice. Even in the worst of conditions, Zoe couldn't sound anything but young.

"What was that?" she whispered. "Were they looking for us?"

"I don't know. I don't think so."

"Then what was it?" Zoe insisted.

"I'm not sure, Zoe…but I don't know if we should stay here." Deep in thought Jonah surveyed his surroundings. *Those bars. Why were there bars if people could slip through them?*

Reaching a decision, Jonah climbed to his feet. "We can't stay here. Let's get back to the tunnel and keep moving."

Jonah extended his hand to pull her up and then lowered her down off the cleft. After scanning the farms, he led her up the gently sloping hill back towards the bars. Jonah was secretly relieved to see them. He didn't want to say anything, but deep down in his gut he knew that whatever was down in the farms was far worse than what was in the tunnels.

Reaching the mouth of the tunnel, Jonah decided it was better for him to scout ahead first. "Wait here Zoe, I'm going to check ahead. If you hear anything, move back down the tunnel. Okay?"

Zoe nodded. Jonah paused for a moment and then slipped through the bars. He walked down the dimly lit tunnels quickly and quietly. He paused, listened, and continued, first down the left tunnel, then down the right. Finding no one, Jonah came back to the entrance to the tunnel.

"It looks clear," he whispered, "but we have to be quiet."

Jonah led Zoe through the bars and to the left. *There had to be someone other than the prisoners left on Mars. If the propaganda over the years was right, there were thousands of miners and scientists here. What could have happened to them? Surely there were others.*

The underground complex was massive. The tunnels twisted and turned with offshoots going both downward and upward. Jonah was afraid to go down lest they return to the farms; and with the farms waited something else, something that necessitated bars. *And for what reason? Why was it trapped? To protect the colony? What were they keeping down there? What had the colonists done?* Considering his options, he suspected the tunnel leading upward might lead to the surface – where they would be cornered. With neither up nor down as an option, he chose to stay on the main tunnel that led away from the landing pad and hopefully towards safety – whatever he expected that salvation to be, he couldn't say.

The sound of voices bouncing off the walls snapped him back to the present. Jonah grabbed Zoe and pulled her backwards. *The tunnel, where was the last tunnel? Behind us.* He turned with Zoe to run, but it was too late. The voices had turned into shapes and they were suddenly trapped, like deer caught in the headlights.

"Hey!" he heard a voice shout behind them.

"Run, hide in the first opening on the right," Jonah ordered in an urgent whisper. Jonah knew that they wouldn't be able to make it by running together, he would have to distract them to give her a chance to hide. Zoe obeyed and took off in a full sprint. Jonah turned to face down the men behind him. Two of them, wearing grey and carrying crudely carved bats, started to jog towards him. As he raised his club he heard a scream followed by a thud behind him. *Zoe!*

Spinning back around Jonah saw her clawing to get up. Behind her were two men in filthy orange jumpsuits. The convicts. Zoe scrambled to her feet and ran back to Jonah. First there were two. Then a third appeared. They walked slowly, apparently unconcerned about approaching quickly. The men all carried clubs wrapped in barbed-wire that casually rested on their shoulders.

As Zoe reached Jonah, he quickly put her behind him, backing her towards the cavern wall. The men in grey slowed to a walk when they saw the convicts. Both parties now approached slowly, stopping to within a few meters of him. Ignoring Jonah and Zoe, the two groups stared at each other.

After a moment, a man in grey pointed the tip of his bat at the convicts and began to speak. Hatred dripped from every word. "You've crossed the line. Go back to where you're authorized to be," he ordered.

As Jonah watched, a man moved smoothly out of the shadows

and crossed in front of the other two men in orange. "We're not leaving without that guy right there."

Jonah realized what was going on – he had been dressed in orange; the garb of a convict. The men in grey must have been the miners. Probably a second camp that came together after the colony collapsed. As Jonah stood with his back to the wall, a pit grew in his stomach. He realized that the miners would rightly consider him a criminal, and not only a criminal, but someone they couldn't possibly trust to bring along.

"We don't want no convict," responded the miner. "You can have him. But who's that with him?"

"We're taking them both. They're from our area and we claim 'em."

"You're not taking that girl. That girl's coming with us," said the second miner.

The convict doing the talking looked over his shoulder at the other two and shrugged.

Are they coming to an agreement over us? The contrast between the two groups was so stark that Jonah knew even Zoe felt the evil dripping from the convict's tongue. They were filthy and covered from head to toe in red dust and grime. The one that spoke was missing globs of hair and had looked as if he was exposed to a nuclear reactor for just a few moments too long. Their hands looked powerful as they gripped the clubs, but were also scarred, with some cuts seeming more recent. In contrast, the miners looked as if they had never swung a club in their life. Their grey jump suits were relatively clean and their faces looked untouched by whatever radioactive energy had saturated the other camp. For some reason that surprised Jonah the most, as if radiation free was an elite social status rather than what should be the norm! Regardless, this wasn't going the direction Jonah had hoped for and without a second thought, he decided it was his turn to talk.

"She's not going anywhere without me, and I'm not coming with you," Jonah said, looking straight at the convicts. Then he turned toward the men in grey. "We are seeking asylum. We just landed and were attacked. Help us… please."

The convict chuckled and the miners looked confused. They must have assumed he was with the convicts at first. After a moment longer one miner whispered something to the other. Jonah strained desperately to hear what they were saying, but he was too far away. Looking back and forth between the miners and the convicts, Jonah was becoming uneasy. Thinking he saw one of the miner's glance at him, he fixed his gaze on them; but quickly realizing this distraction could lead to an attack by the convicts, he shifted back immediately to watch what he thought was the more dangerous of the two groups. The three stood silently in their orange jumpsuits waiting for a decision. It didn't look like the men in orange were going to pick a fight, and Jonah found himself wondering what the agreements of the truce must have been.

Finally, one of the miners spoke. "You can both come with us, you'll be safe." The convicts smile faded and his face became bright red. Then, almost as an afterthought, the miner added, "I have a message for Malek."

Jonah wasn't sure what had just transpired, but he thought they were on the right side. At the gesture of the miners, Jonah moved Zoe down the tunnel. The first miner stepped past him and moved towards the convict. The second led them away. "The name's Chuck," he said as he reached out his hand. Jonah took it and thanked him, but looked back to see the other two talking. *What could they be saying? What message? And who was Malek?*

CHAPTER 30

The main tunnel wound deep into the Martian underground. Jonah couldn't believe how much tunneling had been done as they moved along the twists and turns. Florescent lights were bolted to the ceilings, but otherwise they were surrounded by deep red tunneled rock.

"Thank you again for helping us," Jonah said.

"Not a problem," replied the first, who had caught back up with the group. "It's hard to survive here. We're all in this together."

"What happened here?"

"What happened? This place is hell, that's what happened. Has been for a long time."

"I've seen tourism commercials about this place… it looked nice."

"Oh, they've been lying about this place for years. We get people coming in here, some folks thinking there are jobs, some prisoners, all lied to. This place is a death trap. Most of them don't make it long. The prisoners took control of the landing pad and grab folks as they come in. We do our best to protect the ones that make it to us, but it's not easy. The convicts don't make it easy."

"Why would they lie?" Jonah pondered. "It's been like this for years?"

"You bet. I'll let the head of the colony fill you in on the details. Look, before I bring you into the camp I just want to say, we don't care what you did on Earth. If you're willing to work toward the common good, whatever crimes you're guilty of, we don't care. We just want things to move along peacefully; if you can do that, you'll be welcome to stay."

Jonah made eye contact with the man and nodded. "I won't give you any trouble. I owe you."

"Good," he responded. "We're coming up to the checkpoint. Just let us do the talking."

The checkpoint was little more than a few rusted steel beams angled and stacked in such a way that it would be difficult for an intruder to get through the obstacle and fight off one of the two guards standing behind the barricade. They looked tired. Both of them leaned against the barricade with their bats rested against the walls of the tunnel. As the four approached, one of the men, reacting to Jonah's orange jump suit, climbed off his elbows and picked up his bat. "It's fine, you lazy oaf," shouted Chuck with a smile. The man at the checkpoint lowered his bat but still looked confused. When they finally got closer, Chuck explained the situation and the guards at the checkpoint let the four pass through.

Ahead, the rust red tunnel abruptly ceased. In its place was a set of carved steps that led them upward. Upon reaching the steps, Jonah felt so turned around that he couldn't make sense of up or down. No more than twelve hours ago, he had been hurtling through space at over thirty thousand miles per hour, was shot like a torpedo through the Martian atmosphere into a hanger built underground, had rested in a set of presumably radioactive farms, and raced through tunnels escaping convicts. Now, for all he knew, they were ascending a set of dark red and orange stairs to the surface where his pleasant escort might just open a hatch and allow them to suffocate in the thin Martian air. Understandably, Jonah felt uneasy.

"Where are we going?" Jonah asked.

"This is the Hotel Olympia. The first great hotel of space tourism… and probably the last."

The hallway got brighter the higher they climbed. Not because the artificial lights had changed but because windows suddenly appeared. They were rising above the surface and could now see the entirety of the Martian landscape. Sand covered hills rolled away from the hotel while mountains stretched upwards reaching towards the sky. It was beautiful, but completely desolate. There was no life out there. Jonah felt covered with dread. *How could he possibly get off this planet?* As they climbed higher, the hotel felt more like a mausoleum than a sanctuary. This was a place that would mark their deaths. He would die alone on this barren planet without friends or family. Buried in the belly of Mars forever.

Eventually, the stairway ended and they found themselves entering a large lobby. Jonah estimated they were about three stories above the Martian surface now. Looking over at Zoe, he found relief washing over her features. She looked up at Jonah and smiled. In her mind, they had made it to safety.

The lobby exuded a ghostly reminder of what it once was – remnants of futuristic elegance with a mix of childhood space exploration wonder. Now it more closely resembled a Midwest saloon – its former glory faded and tattered. Dust blanketed the once-shined floors and coated the large picture frame windows elegantly placed to overlook the Martian landscape below. The walls were a light grey and metallic sculptures of hallowed out squares and circular planetary orbits decorated the walls and were propped on the various end tables throughout the room. Besides light that shone through the windows, a bright florescent glow emanated from alcoves in the white ceiling above providing an attempted sterilized look at the dust covered floor below. The metallic chairs, curved to resemble the form of a person, were scuffed and the padded head cushion was worn, but people sat in them reading books and chatting aimlessly.

The shiniest part of the whole reception area was a bar to the left, where patrons gathered hoping to drown their boredom in a pool of brandy or vodka. A young woman stood behind the counter wearing an apron with a beige rag tossed casually over her shoulder. Jonah couldn't help but laugh to himself. Where there are people, there is alcohol. Some things never change.

As they walked deeper into the lobby, people put their books down and turned from the bar. In his orange jumpsuit holding a club still fresh with blood, Jonah imagined they must have thought the worst of him. In their minds, a convict had just entered their sanctuary.

Bringing his focus back to what was ahead of him, he saw a short, plump woman pumping her arms briskly as she hurried down the lobby stairs. Tossing a fake smile at Jonah, she sternly looked at his escort.

"Take that club from him," she hissed sharply. "He's got everyone in here all worked up."

The escort put out his hand and apologetically looked at Jonah. Jonah diplomatically relinquished the club and feigned a smile of his own. The patrons of the bar, wide eyed in anticipation of a stray convict attacking security guards, shrugged their shoulders, let out a yawn, and returned to their drinks and small talk. It was strange how simple it was to get everyone uninterested in him again. Were they so under-stimulated that the only visitor they hoped for was one that would club the plump lady to death like a gladiator in an arena? Were they really so unimpressed with the lack of violence that they didn't care who he was, they just preferred a good show? The girl behind the bar poured a patron a shot of whiskey, which he took immediately by throwing his head back then slamming the glass back onto the table to ask for more. If there was not going to be a murderous convict clubbing people to death in the bar, then they would get drunk. That much was obvious.

"Jillian Jaspers," the woman said abruptly, sticking out her hand.

Jillian Jaspers. A legend that had her pudgy face scattered across countless American malls, and was embodied in numerous books and movies, was personally greeting him on Mars. Jonah couldn't believe he now stood face-to-face with the woman that had spurred such imagination and creativity. Of course he would never say it, but despite his surprise at meeting the pioneer of modern space exploration, he had hoped to feel more awe. He didn't. Five months of sleep followed by brutally beating four convicts to death seemed to trump meeting the star scientist. Instead, Jonah took her hand and greeted her warmly, "Jonah Shepherd," he said, "and this is Zoe."

She smiled at Zoe briefly but then looked back to Jonah. "You have a lot of explaining to do if you expect to stay here." Turning, she gestured for him to follow her. Jonah took Zoe by the hand and smiled at her. Jillian snapped her fingers at someone reclining on the couch. "Find this girl a room and some clean clothes. Tell me where you put her."

Zoe looked up at Jonah to see if he was okay with her leaving and he nodded. "I'll be back in a few minutes. They'll take me to you when I'm finished speaking with Jillian."

In awkward silence, Jillian led Jonah behind the stairs into a back hallway. It wasn't entirely silent. Her short, choppy steps and larger-than-jump-suit-authorized thighs caused a 'swish swash' all the way down the hall. Offices lined both sides. Two large men in grey jumpsuits followed closely behind him. He sensed that she didn't trust him, and occasionally she would turn her head just enough to watch him out of the corner of her eye. It was obvious, of course, but Jonah was happy to see they took security seriously and felt more at ease with leaving Zoe to find her room. At last, they reached an office at the end of the hallway. Unlocking the door, she gestured for him to sit down and after moving around the desk, Jillian plopped her plump body into her chair and stared at him for a moment.

"I want to be frank with you, Jonah," she started. "I don't trust you." She twirled her chair to the side and adjusted her pants. They swished and swashed as she scooted her butt up in the chair and her pants down. The chair creaked as she shifted side to side. Everything about Jillian seemed awkward and uncomfortable. Finally, she turned back around to face Jonah. Clasping her hands together near her face, she reminded Jonah of a *James Bond* villain. "If you and Zoe want to stay here you're going to have to do something for us."

Jonah didn't say anything. He assumed there would be as much. The two camps more resembled a gang a community. And gangs always had rites of initiation.

"When our scouts came back and reported what they saw you do in the landing pod, at first, I didn't believe it. I couldn't imagine anyone taking on four convicts. But now I can see for myself and I believe. So tell me… why were you sent here?"

It always came back to trust, but Jonah felt he could use his chance to speak in a way that gave him an advantage. Everything he did, every relationship he made, every word he uttered had to be deliberate and specific. Beginning his story, he hoped telling her the truth would give her the trust he needed. He told her that he was a soldier, about the wars that he had fought in, and what Earth was like now. Some wars she remembered and asked about their outcome. Others she hadn't heard of. More importantly, Jonah told her about Evangeline and their kids. He told her how desperately he wanted to see them and how he was wrongly convicted at a sham trial in the middle of the night. This seemed to be something she was particularly interested in.

"Sham trial?" she asked, probably trying to determine if he was "innocent" just like every other convict on this God-forsaken planet or if he was actually innocent.

"It's different from when you remember, Jillian." He responded. "How old were you when you left? Twenty-six?" She didn't respond, but by her expression he could see that he was right. There was also a tinge of animosity that formed on her face when he suggested she was young when she left and wasn't tuned in now. Jonah didn't care; one of the perks of age and experience was to tell everyone else how little they knew. Jonah took advantage of it.

"Of course you probably wouldn't have been tuned in, but even back in the 20s, right before you departed, were the clear protests of states proposing separation from the federal government. After my military service, I was hired as an advisor to the governor of Virginia to address what many viewed as a dangerous shift in both domestic and foreign policy. Wars over resources were suddenly *economically viable* and anyone in the country that dissented or failed to contribute to the new effort was considered a waste of national resources. The congress split in two and many congressmen and senators no longer traveled to the capital. It's truly a dark time, Jillian."

"You've given me everything but your explanation of innocence," she reminded him.

Her words peeled off her mouth in a dry and witless tone. Regardless, Jonah thought it was right to answer her because of the hospitality she had thus far given them. "I didn't realize how much surveillance the government was performing on its own people. During my trial they played recordings of my interactions with the governor and other officials that opposed the party line. I was deemed an enemy of the state and found guilty of treason."

"Which you admit to doing?"

Jonah could tell where she was going. The charge was treason and, to her, he was guilty. "The government has no right to restrict political gatherings. We retain our first amendment and have the right to not only disagree, but to gather together, protest our grievances, and demand reform," Jonah responded sternly.

Jillian leaned back in her chair and turned around towards her window, obviously deep in thought.

After what seemed like an eternity of weighty silence, she turned back to Jonah. Although he couldn't be sure, it looked like her eyes were wet. She blinked once, twice, and instantly any vulnerability he thought he saw had vaporized. Looking directly into his eyes, she spoke.

"Jonah, we've been living like this for months now," she said. The shift of topic caught him off guard and left him slightly alarmed. "The camps are divided in two. There was an earthquake about seven months ago that caused an oxygen processing unit to explode in the marines' living quarters, killing hundreds. That same earthquake ripped the inner walls of the prison apart. The marines that didn't die from the blast were left to fight off Earth's worst convicts. Overmatched and under-supplied, the few marines that had survived the initial onslaught from the convicts died in the following days, either in the tunnels, or by starving to death where they barricaded themselves.

On our side of the colony, the earthquake damaged most of our vital systems and collapsed a lot of the mines. By the time we got the atmosphere back under control, we realized that the colony was in chaos. Miners were trapped, the marines were caught entirely off guard, and our communication systems were in disarray. The prisoners had seized weapons and were executing everyone they could find that wasn't wearing orange. We barricaded ourselves on this end of the tunnel with the help of the remaining miners."

Jillian shifted in her chair and intuited his next question. "If there was ever a distress call, nobody heard it. The convicts destroyed the surface vehicles and sealed themselves in. Anytime they want something, they raid our farms and water stores. Don't get me wrong, we've held our own. We have plenty of food and water, and we have even engaged in some diplomacy with the prison camp. We've done what we can to defend ourselves, but the people here aren't soldiers." Jillian paused to take a sip of water. "About three months ago, the criminals changed tactics. In addition to stealing our resources, they also began to steal our young women. I can't imagine the horrible things they are doing to them. Just last night, another one of our girls was kidnapped."

Jonah knew what she was getting ready to ask. In order to be granted asylum, she wanted him to get the girl back. In his mind he was still trying to piece the situation together. *Why couldn't Earth have learned the truth? No communication for seven months and they continue to send ships? Aren't the corporations worried? Why are the convicts stealing women?*

"I need you to bring the girl back to me," Jillian declared, breaking his thoughts. "If you do this, you can stay here as long as you want. I don't care who you were on Earth as long as you can be trusted here. This is how you will prove to me that I can trust you."

So that was the deal. Sneak into an enemy camp and bring back a prisoner. It certainly wasn't the most dangerous thing he'd ever done; but it wasn't the least dangerous either. Jonah looked down at his hands and forearms. There was still some dried blood that had splattered onto his sleeves from the fight back at the hanger. When he was discharged from the Army a sense of relief flooded him. Now, that relief could not be farther away. It was entirely out of reach, and mentally claw as he would like, he knew that both his past memories and the ones he was about to forge would forever torment him. "I'll get her back for you," Jonah responded. "But I expect you to help me get off Mars."

Jillian laughed. "We all want off Mars, Jonah! Why do you think we're still here? Nobody cares about us enough to launch a rescue mission and the companies we work for have all but abandoned us." She paused again. "Jonah, when I led the very first expedition to Mars, the corporation I represented said something that I will never forget. Instead of saying 'goodbye,' 'we're proud of you,' or some other farewell, they said 'if things go bad up there, we won't come get you.' It's that simple Jonah. We are on our own."

Jonah frowned. He wanted to ask why the corporations were still sending people. Something wasn't adding up, but he could tell she didn't trust him enough to divulge the truth. He would have to work his way into her trust. "You have my word that I will bring the girl back," he responded. "But I want yours as well. I get the girl, you get me home." She didn't respond, so Jonah prodded her for pity. "Come on, Jillian, there has to be a way to get out of here. All I want is to get back to my family. That's it."

"Okay," Jillian said. "There might be a way," and leaning forward she quietly added, "But you have to take me with you."

Jonah nodded and Jillian motioned for the two guards to come forward. "Bring him back to Zoe. Get him a shower and a clean jumpsuit." She looked at Jonah. "The planet goes dark in eight hours. Once you're ready we'll meet in my office to show you the plan. In the meantime, you can visit the food court and enjoy the sights."

CHAPTER 31

Logan Carter awoke to flashing red lights and the sound of sirens. Hearing the sounds but not truly comprehending its meaning, he laid on the concrete floor for a moment longer. His eyes hurt to look around, and his head ached worse than after a night of binge drinking. Logan strained to remember exactly what had just happened. The power had come back on, but *who had attacked him? And why was the power turned off in the first place?* As the haze cleared from his mind and his vision, things became clearer.

In all of Logan's time working here he had never heard the siren or the alarm that was now playing. An automated voice screamed at him over the PA system. "Nuclear Warhead - Armed." It repeated again and again. Those words finally hit home like a Mack truck smashing into a shopping cart. "Nuclear Warhead - Armed." *This can't be happening.*

Logan rolled over onto his knees and pushed himself to his feet. His stomach ached and his head throbbed. Suddenly, he found himself wishing he had spent more time working out in the gym instead of eating crunchy Cheetos. Steadying himself for a moment before attempting to get to his desk, the world spun violently around him. He took a step, stumbled over his own feet and fell. The alarm boomed. "Nuclear Warhead - Armed."

Once a sequence was initiated, there was no way to turn the warhead off remotely. On his hands and knees again, Logan eyed the twisted steel door that had been blown to pieces by whatever explosives the team used to get inside. To disarm the nuclear weapon, Logan knew he had to make his way down the quarter mile hallway and twenty-two floors of empty hangar that housed the skyscraper height ballistic missiles. Crawling back to his feet and steadying himself on the edge of his desk, he staggered towards the opening in the door. His legs wobbled, but with each step he could feel his muscles strengthen; then the alarm changed, a new message was broadcast, and fear mixed with adrenaline surged to strengthen his weary legs. "Five minutes until nuclear detonation - Five minutes until nuclear detonation."

Five minutes, not much time. "I'm not going to die here," Logan muttered to himself as he finally reached the door. Sparks flew from the electrical wires severed by the blast and steam hissed from the hydraulic lines responsible for opening the doors. "I'm not going to die here," he said again, attempting to motivate his terribly out of shape body to cross the threshold and break into a jog. Every fiber of his being craved to live, but he could not quite figure out why. He had accomplished nothing. He lived alone. He survived on Cheetos and diet Coke, and the hours he spent not at work were either spent sleeping or watching dirty movies from his couch, waiting to pass out from exhaustion in the hopes that his alarm would wake him up and he would remember nothing from the previous night. In that moment, Logan could honestly look himself in the mirror and see that his life had truly been wasted. And yet, he drove on.

"Four minutes until nuclear detonation," the voice howled. Logan turned left down the corridor toward the missile bay, saw a dead guard and almost vomited, catching himself on the far wall. Adrenaline surged through him, but his muscles had nothing to fuel themselves off of but empty carbohydrates and caffeine. Shaky and weak, Logan pressed on, averting his eyes from the not one, but over a dozen bodies lifelessly littering the tunnel toward the missile bay. Although red lights still flashed along the walls, the florescent lights lining the hallway of his concrete tunnel flickered on and off. This area was apparently less affected by whatever the attackers used to turn off their systems.

"Three minutes until nuclear detonation." Logan was exhausted rushing down hallways and tunnels towards the missile bay. *Why the hell would anyone put the two sections so far apart? Didn't they realize that if someone had to manually disarm a nuclear weapon they would have to get there quickly? Who was the moron that built this underground complex?* Logan hoped his anger would energize him further, but the pain in his side only intensified as he pressed onward. All of the action movies he had watched about ordinary men doing extraordinary things during extreme circumstances appeared to be dead wrong. He was still incapable of running anything faster than a fifteen minute mile, his breath still smelled like Cheetos, and his stomach was empty of any fuel that could have kept him going.

Logan stopped at the elevator leading to the bottom of the missile bay and pressed the button, once, twice, and a third time. The elevator didn't light up. Even with his recent surge of adrenaline he dreaded having to acknowledge that he would have to further exert himself on the stairs. *Thank God I am going downstairs instead of up.*

Flying down the stairs at max speed, the voice gave its second-to-last announcement. "Two minutes until nuclear detonation." Logan went into hyper drive, skipping one, two, three stairs at a time leaping and bounding down them. "I'm not going to die!" he shouted, begging his body to push faster and harder than it ever had before. He stumbled down the last few stairs, flew through the door leading to the bottom of the missile bay and to the computer hard wired to the nuclear missile, tripped on his own feet but rolled like a superhero, pushed himself onto his feet again, and finally reached the computer station.

For the first time, he realized it was possible there were armed men still in the bunker to ensure everything went the way it should, but he was relieved to find it was only him and the deceased bodies of his colleagues. Logan reached his key card still stuck in the computer just in time to be informed: "One minute to nuclear detonation." One more minute, and they all became free-floating particles. Dripping sweat all over the computer screen, Logan pressed his code onto the keyboard, twisted his key card back to the "disarm" position and collapsed to the ground in complete exhaustion.

Logan leaned against the back of the computer stand for a moment trying to catch his breath. He couldn't believe it. Raising his hand to his face to wipe the sweat from his brow he noticed they were shaking. Thirty seconds was the difference between life and death. He looked over towards the missiles. The missiles. They were missing. Logan's heart sank, and a cold panicked sweat once again coated his forehead. So it wasn't over. Some of the missiles must have been launched.

CHAPTER 32

By the time his scouts returned, Malek was enjoying dinner and some entertainment. Malek laughed and giggled while shoving a glowing and potentially radioactive broccoli into his mouth. In the center of the floor, below his throne chair, were two German shepherds taken from the dead prison guards during the rebellion. Fighting the length of their leashes, the dogs lunged forward, snapping their jaws again and again. Between the dogs was the girl that should have been eaten hours ago. Behind her, a man with a whip drove her towards the dogs. Jumping to escape the whip she landed within range of deadly sharp teeth. Lunging forward, the dog would snap its jaws at her, only to be pulled back by its handler. The game continued. The snap of a whip, a scream, the sharp clack of teeth just barely out of reach of the terrified girl.

Sitting on this throne, Malek enjoyed the show; hoping the handler's grip would slip, even if only a little. Eventually, with a sigh of disappointment, Malek dismissed the girl back to her cage and turned his attention to his scout.

"Well?" he said, staring blankly at the scout.

"We found him. He made it to the miner's camp."

Malek grimaced. After spending the afternoon thinking about the events that had transpired, and at the advice of his generals, he had decided he wanted to bring the new convict back and give him an opportunity to join their camp. Anyone who could kill four of his men would be a real asset. The scout started to speak again but he was silenced by the raising of Malek's index finger. He pondered a bit further. Reaching down, Malek grabbed an apple off the plate and sunk his pointed teeth through the skin. Juices ran down his jaw, forming a drop on the bottom of his chin. He wiped it away with his forearm and spoke to the scout, mouth full and spitting while he talked.

"Did you have something else?"

"The scientist has a message for you," the scout replied.

Malek balked. "She has something for me?!" He sank his teeth into the apple again. This time, the juice ran down his chin and onto his neck. The sores on his face moved up and down while he chewed. Puss oozed from one of his larger sores and joined the juice from his apple at the corner of his mouth.

Unsure whether or not to proceed, the scout started, then

stopped, then started again. "She wants the girl back and is willing to trade."

"Trade?!" He shouted back at the scout. "She doesn't have anything I want!"

The scout started again, but he was cut off. "I take what I want! She has no right to ask for anything!" Malek slumped back into his chair. "After what they've done to us?! They are lucky I even let her exist!"

"Malek, please forgive me, but I have to tell you the rest of the message." Malek flamboyantly exaggerated the wave of his hand and the scout continued. "The guard told me she threatened to release the grootslang if you wouldn't negotiate with her."

With an attitude of nonchalance, he motioned for the scout to leave his presence. *The grootslang. She doesn't have the guts, she couldn't control that genetic monstrosity enough to make it effective.* From the corner of his eye he could see his generals whispering to each other. Now was not the time to look weak.

CHAPTER 33

Emergency sirens filled the city, but most people went about their daily business as if no siren screamed at all. It wouldn't have mattered if they took cover, which few, if any, did, because in an effort to avoid mass panic the Department of Homeland Security avoided sounding the alarm signaling an impending attack until just a few minutes before impact. This, coupled with the fact that the thermonuclear weapon had a blast radius of about twenty miles left no hope for those hiding in their homes or shopping in the square.

On this particular Friday morning, with the sun shining and fluffy clouds floating through the rich blue sky, the president had gathered various media outlets on the white house lawn to discuss the nuances of the separatist movements and to justify his preemptive attack.

"We attacked them because it was clear they were repositioning their bomber fleet to conduct strikes on their own soil and against their own countrymen!" he declared with a smash of his fist on the podium. The sticking point that he wanted everyone to hear and understand was that his government was fair and transparent, and that the grounds on which the so-called Free States complained were illegitimate and exaggerated.

Charlie Miller watched the speech from the comfort of his home, far from the capital in Washington State. While Charlie understood politics, he wasn't sure if the president's speech was more politics or lies. There was no repositioning of bomber fleets. There hadn't been anything of the sort. Charlie understood the pre-emptive strike for what it was. To pre-empt the potential of the moving of bomber fleets. To send a message to the separatist states that they were not in control of their airfields, and the federal government would take the required steps to send that message. To keep the country united. And lastly, to reduce the combat power of those who would like to fracture that relationship.

Ordinarily, Charlie would be at work today. Given the events of the last seventy-two hours, however, he had been placed on leave until the investigation into the raid had been completed. Charlie reclined back in his brown leather lazy boy and took another sip from his bottle of Sam Adams. If he was going to be honest with himself, he didn't mind the leave. The guilt he felt after the operation, both for his soldier and for attacking his fellow countrymen, was overwhelming and made him even rethink his purpose in life.

Throughout Charlie's military career, he had been praised for his dependability. He was called a team player, loyal, dedicated to his mission. Now he felt like a pawn. Someone who acted without a conscious moral thought and was too spineless to stand up for himself. He took another sip from his beer and focused on the TV. Something was happening. A red news alert scrolled along the bottom of the screen. Three beers into his morning, however, and Charlie had trouble reading the words. He could see the live feed, and it was telling.

The president appeared to be so intent on making his point that he was fighting off almost a dozen secret service agents at the podium. With the microphone still on, Charlie, and the rest of the country could hear words like "credible threat" and "danger to your life." His ears perked up. *Was this something in response to his operation?* The cameras continued to capture the president's secret service agents literally dragging him from the podium, across the white house yard, and then out of view.

Charlie sat up in his chair and staggered drunkenly over to the table where he thought he left his cell phone. Unable to find the phone, he wandered back into the living room, sunk back into his chair, and continued watching the news. But instead of the national news station, a local one had appeared, and showed a middle-aged balding man frantically reading off warnings to the general public.

"To reiterate," he said, apparently for the second time, "no one should leave their homes. Take shelter in a basement, a subway station, or even under a bridge. Anything that can protect you from the blast." *Blast?* "It is still unclear where the missiles originated from… wait… I'm just getting word that the United States has apparently counter-fired with missiles of its own… we don't know if they were nuclear in nature." *Nuclear?* Charlie looked down at his beer as if to examine whether or not it was laced with illicit drugs. "Again, three warheads have launched from an Air Force base in North Dakota targeting two US cities: Washington DC and Los Angeles. And we suspect one missile is headed for Beijing. May God be with everyone in our two countries." The anchor then turned to his counterpart who was standing near a large map attempting to illustrate the potential fallout.

Charlie didn't want to hear any more. He knew all too well about the fallout and searched feverishly for his phone. *This couldn't be happening.*

****

Three thousand miles away and sitting in a coffee shop in the District of Columbia, Clark had no problem propagating mass panic as soon as the sirens across the city erupted in a deep whine. Clark didn't consider himself a coward, but he didn't consider himself stupid, either. Clark had watched enough movies to know that whenever a city-wide siren blasted the next thing to follow would be a nuclear blast, or a tsunami, a tornado, or maybe even Godzilla and King Kong. Clark didn't care what it was; he just wanted to find safety.

Shooting out of his chair, and somewhat surprised to be the first one to stand in a room full of nose-pierced coffee lovers, Clark took one final swig of his Caramel Macchiato, savored the flavored whipped cream lining the lip of his cup, grabbed his tablet, and ran out of the shop, his black and white striped ear phones dangling against the side of his leg while he ran. Two girls at the far end of restaurant snickered when he rushed out in a frenzy, but he didn't care. After the work he had been doing, there was nothing to laugh about.

The street was far busier than the coffee shop; at least some people were heeding the sirens, unlike than his fellow espresso drinkers inside. On the busy sidewalk, pedestrians scurried about, shoving and shouldering Clark to get past him.

"What's going on?" Clark shouted at a group holding each other as they ran past. The group looked up at him for less than a second before continuing on. As Clark surveyed the crowd and tried to determine whether to find high ground for a tsunami, or shelter from a tornado, he had trouble not noticing his handiwork. Even in the district, Clark's posters and billboards blaming the Free States for the downfall of the nation and recruiting young men and women to be soldiers to defend against any Free State aggression were prevalent. They had even erected a new one that blamed the Free States for a cross border strike.

Just as he was getting ready to choose the high ground to avoid an asteroid-caused-tsunami, a voice interrupted the sirens. "Take shelter immediately," the male's voice alerted. "Nuclear strike is imminent. Take shelter immediately."

Nuclear Strike? The voice wouldn't have to say immediately to Clark ever again. Gripping his tablet tightly, Clark pushed through the crowd, looking for the nearest subway station. In D.C., he only had to go a block or two. Or was it three? He couldn't remember, but didn't care. As Clark ran, he noticed one last piece of his work that would soon be disintegrated. It was a billboard at the top of the square and contained a picture of genetically modified crops with the words "Repairing Even the Most Damaged Ecosystems." Beneath its slogan was the familiar Unicore logo - four red triangles arranged to form a square in the center. Clark wasn't certain he believed any of his advertising, but suddenly in the face of the very real disaster, Clark found comfort in the hope that even this city could be repaired as a result of modern science.

The voice repeated its warning as the siren blared. Apparently the government cared less about mass panic than a nuclear detonation because the previous alert sent the already concerned street into complete chaos. Pedestrians turned into maniacs crashing through store front windows and carrying out water. Slower families with small children were being pushed and shoved. Clark was appalled, but not appalled enough to stop and help. In fact, he was surprised to find a feeling of gratefulness erupt inside of him. These families wouldn't make it. They would either be stuck on the street or starve in the aftermath. Clark was alone. He only had himself to think about.

Finally reaching the entrance of the subway, Clark rounded the corner and found himself crammed inside a wall of people shoving and shouting to get down the stairs. Sweat poured from his forehead. *How soon was imminent? How fast did the voice mean when it said immediately? How long had it been? Five, ten minutes?* The crowd was moving too slowly. There were too many people. He continued to sweat, but his forehead became cold. His hands were clammy. His face felt flush. This couldn't be it. This couldn't be. Babies cried and children hung anxiously onto their parents as they descended deeper into the subway system.

Finally at the bottom, the crowd dispersed onto the platform directed by subway officials and police officers. Clark jumped down to the tracks finding a seat against the wall and waited… and waited. Then the ground shook.

CHAPTER 34

By the time Jonah returned to Zoe, she had already discovered the shower and clean set of jumpsuits that hung in the closet of the hotel room. She now sat on a chair hugging her knees to her chest and stared out a large window overlooking the stunning Martian landscape. The sun, a much smaller dot in the light red sky, hung at about the three o'clock position. Jonah tried to think about what his family would be doing in the midafternoon, but for the life of him, he couldn't remember if it was a work day or weekend.

"Well?" Zoe asked, not turning around.

Jonah let the door close behind him as he stepped farther into the room. The layout was similar to any standard motel room on earth. A small bathroom containing a sink, toilet, and shower was on his left, near the door. The walls opened up past the bathroom to reveal two queen sized beds tucked in further to his left and a television atop a small dresser to his right. The room was carpeted in soft cream and the walls glowed a rich caramel brown. Despite being in prison for months, Jonah couldn't help but feel disappointed at the early twenty-first century ambiance. But because of travel time and resources, he assumed the real architectural feat was accomplished on the outside of the hotel to withstand the Martian weather and radioactive waves penetrating its weaker magnetic field.

Jonah looked back at Zoe. "It seems like we are safe here," he replied. There were two large paintings hanging above each bed. One was a perspective painting from a satellite orbiting earth. The second was the mars rover examining a rock. The paintings neither matched the color scheme, nor seemed elegant enough to use as décor in a space hotel. Nonetheless, Jonah found himself staring at them blankly expecting some revelation to magically appear the longer he stared at the art. Nothing came to him, and he eventually turned back to Zoe. "How are you doing?"

"How do you think?" she retorted, more exhausted than angry.

Jonah moved around to her right side and tried to look at her face but she turned it just enough as to examine something on the mountain to left. "I'm sorry for everything you've been through." He paused. "I can't imagine what you're feeling right now."

Zoe didn't respond, but he didn't really expect her to. Losing parents in such a horrific way was enough to devastate a child;

losing parents after a five-month journey to Mars was enough to absolutely obliterate one.

"Are you hungry? Jillian said there is a food court downstairs."

Zoe shook her head no. Jonah decided he wasn't terribly hungry either, but he knew he should eat to regain his strength. After looking once more at the paintings, he turned to leave her alone when he heard her sobbing. There was no use comforting the girl, and he wouldn't have wanted to be comforted either. He simply sat down on the bed. Finally, Zoe turned her chair toward him and gave the slightest smile. "Since I have no reason to be here now, how do we get back home?" She asked.

Jonah didn't know. He didn't know anything. After the conversation with Jillian, Mars, itself, was only shrouded in greater mystery than ever before. One question rattled louder than any of the others. *Why were companies still sending miners and their families to Mars almost a year after abandoning the mining program?*

"I'm going to do some exploring Zoe," Jonah said looking in her direction. "Will you be okay here until I get back?"

Zoe nodded and wiped her eyes before swiveling the chair back to the window to stare out across the Martian landscape.

"Do you want me to bring anything back for you?" he asked once more.

Zoe didn't respond. As he closed the door and entered the hallway, Jonah recalled Jane's statement on the ship. *Contact Icarus on channel 32.* He would have to find a working radio; one that Jillian claimed no longer existed.

CHAPTER 35

As Mars went black, so did the tunnels. For whatever reason, the lights that powered the network of tunnels twisting and turning beneath the Martian surface had apparently not been connected to batteries capable of holding a charge through the night. Thus, the solar energy was just enough to power them during the day, but without the shining sun, they shut off until the next morning. The tunnels weren't completely dark, however. At random intervals faint streaks of green lined the walls at about chest height. It was as if someone had broken a glow stick and splashed the contents across the walls.

Jonah knew the dim green light emitting from whatever had dried along the cavern walls was not glow sticks. He was not so naïve and his hair prickled when he dared consider it further. The streaks looked more like saliva, the way silver bands of slobber looks when a dog rests its jowls on the couch cushions after drinking a gallon of water. They were disgusting, but Jonah couldn't resist his desire to examine them further. Upon closer inspection, the green streaks had a slight sparkle. Raising his hand, Jonah brought it close to the wall, hesitated, and then swiped the rock with his thumb and index finger. It rubbed off like chalk, and as he moved it back and forth, it lightly flaked off his fingers and drifted down to the ground.

Wiping his hands against the new grey jumpsuit, Jonah found himself gripping his knife even more tightly as he continued down the tunnels. Jillian was kind enough to have given him a long bowie knife for his journey tonight; although he suddenly feared the knife wasn't big enough to handle whatever had left the glowing green light along the tunnel walls. A seasoned warrior, Jonah wasn't given easily to fright, but in these darkened tunnels he couldn't help but let his imagination go wild. *What genetic monstrosity or slimy tunnel creature could have left those marks?*

Even with the light and his own genetic alterations that had enhanced his eyesight, hearing, and muscular reflexes, Jonah found it difficult to see. In Iraq, they cleared underground bunkers and tunnels that Al Qaeda used to move men, weapons, and equipment through districts. The tunnels were so dark, insurgents would literally bump into each other as they tried to find their way through. Night vision enabled soldiers to conduct super human feats back then. They could see into the depths of the darkest tunnels and take advantage of any situation. You never went into a fight intending to play fair – but without his equipment, Jonah would have to improvise, relying on a bowie knife, the darkness, and his experience.

Jonah inched along the passage. Jillian had shown him a map but would not let him take it with him. He understood, and in this darkness, he wouldn't have been able to read it anyway. Jonah had done his best to commit it to memory; a useful skill he picked up throughout his busy career. There were two main tunnels: the one he had first come in on which led to the hangar and eventually the other camp, and the one he traveled on now. According to Jillian, this was a direct route to the camp, but more specifically, to the prison where she thought the girl was being held.

Every so often, Jonah stopped and listened for anything that didn't sound like Mars. Of course, he had no clue what Mars sounded like, but right now it didn't sound like anything, so he listened for voices to warn him if something was coming. Of course the *something* he referred to was something human. If, however, the something happened to be the creature in the farms, the creature he was deathly afraid of, and the monster he was convinced would make short work of him if the two of them ever met, then he probably wouldn't hear it until it was too late and therefore, didn't really need to be listening for it. Instead, he focused on what he knew, and what he knew were humans. Humans were loud, and noisy, and proud. And that is what gave them away.

After an hour or so of walking, he reached a T intersection.

This was one of two intersections he would pass before he had to move down into the farms – the part of the journey he feared the most. Jonah was convinced that whatever had been moving in the farms when he and Zoe were hiding was the same thing that made the glowing saliva-like streaks along the walls of the tunnel. Despite his previous pledge to himself to ignore the things that were non-human, the creature crept back into his imagination and with it, all the terror and dread of the next step of his journey. Jonah walked slower – not to be more careful, but to prolong the last awful moments of his life on Mars should he become food for the *something*.

Despite his stalling, Jonah finally reached the downward-sloping tunnel that led to the farms underneath the convict's camp. The temperature dropped significantly in the cool night air. Carbon dioxide seeping through the rocks from the thin Martian atmosphere dripped down the cavern wall. Fog formed quickly and stirred around his feet as he walked. In the green hue of the genetically enhanced plants, the fog looked like clouds of chlorine gas dancing lazily about. Jonah crouched while he moved, and worked quickly to circumvent the plants. He was looking for the second tunnel on his right but in the low lying fog it was extremely difficult to find.

Suddenly, a hiss filled the chamber. Jonah dropped to the ground and rolled towards the wall, scraping his forearm against the rocky Martian ground. Climbing to his knees to see above the fog, he scanned the plants in the center of the chamber. In the dim green light, it was impossible to see beyond the first row of crops. *The something made that hiss!* And then, it made another one. The deep hiss came into the chamber as violently as the first. The thick stems on the genetically enhanced crop swayed suddenly. Jonah remained frozen, plastered against the cold cavern wall. He waited in silence for ten minutes, then he decided it was safe enough to continue on his trek. As he crept forward, the plants remained still and the fog only gently swirled around his feet. Finding a tunnel to his left, he ducked inside and was happy to be going upward. *There is something terribly wrong with those farms.*

CHAPTER 36

It swayed back and forth for her. That giant worm. Experiment gone wrong. Its sharp, snake-like tongue jutted in and out of its wide circular mouth. Saliva dripped off rows of razor sharp teeth as it waited, mouth open for the gift she was preparing to give. It didn't need meat – she'd designed it to survive on sulfur and iron found beneath the surface. But it liked meat. And she was happy to oblige.

Guards led two blindfolded miners down the narrow passageway. The worm, standing on its tail, leaned towards them and hissed like a cobra ready to strike. It was a quiet hiss, almost a purr, and as soon as it let out its purr, the worm shrunk below the ledge and wrapped itself upward around a cavern stalactite to increase its reach. The miners pleaded. She ignored them, instead choosing to remove their blindfolds so they could watch her majestic creation consume them. Helpless and vulnerable, the two were put on their knees at the mouth of the cavern and they whimpered softly as the giant worm unwrapped itself and slithered along the ground to stand in front of them. Reaching its favored location, the worm rose up, extending its body to full height far above the thin ledge that served as its feeding tray. Smiling, she turned as she ascended back up the passage way to the sound of desperate screams followed by complete silence.

CHAPTER 37

At last, Jonah made it to the final stretch. In the darkness he could see light radiating from the fissure in the rock wall. According to Jillian, this was the fissure that the convicts had used to escape after the earthquake. Jonah was relieved to see it. He had expected to see the guards on the other side of the wall. The very thought of other humans compared to whatever was living in those farms was refreshing, even knowing he would probably have to kill them.

As he crept closer, Jonah could hear their banter. One laughed loudly as the other spoke. They were relaxed and preoccupied; exactly as Jonah had hoped. Up against the wall, he inched towards the fissure. Reaching its center, Jonah slowly peered through. There were two guards, both sitting on stools and both facing inwards towards the cell. Between them was a lantern. Beyond the two men were the bars that held their only prisoner; the girl stolen a few nights earlier.

Light from the lantern flame danced back and forth illuminating the girl's face as she huddled against the far wall of cell. Jonah found himself wrought with pity for her. He couldn't help but think back to his daughter Eden, and as he did, the familiar pit grew in his stomach until it became a stone. Her torment hit too close to home and the stone twisted inside his belly until it became fury. In the last twenty-four hours, Jonah had seen raw evil. Without provocation, this evil had snatched the parents from Zoe, and now, it threatened to tear through the heart of this other girl. Her expression looked tormented, but at the same time, empty. She had nothing left and her face revealed she expected death.

"What do you think she'll do if I do this?" The one said to the other.

Jonah watched as he took an iron rod and held it to the lantern's flame. After it was glowing, he put it through the bars and laid it against the girl's bare legs. She screamed and both men laughed. Anger rose within him, and before he knew it, he was through the fissure wall.

Jonah targeted the man with the pole first; assuming he posed the greatest risk. Before they knew what was happening, he was on them. With his right hand, he shoved the bowie knife's fourteen-inch blade through the man's back and lifted him off his feet. The guard let out a gasp of air as blood poured from his chest onto the ground. Still connected to the first guard but within reach of the second, Jonah swept with his left leg, kicking the stool out from under him. The man fell flat on his back and hit the ground hard. Jonah twisted the knife out, and pounced on the dying man's fallen comrade, punching the knife through his neck with such speed and strength that he never stood a chance. In less than a few seconds it was over.

Jonah paused before pulling his knife out, but in that moment, he realized his mistake. The guards were in the middle of a shift change. Rushing down the stairs were four more, then two behind them. Before he could stand, the first group lunged at him like brawlers. Side stepping, he slashed the first one's stomach and ducked the swing of a bat. The bars vibrated and clanged as it bounced off the cage. But they had surrounded him. Another one swung and missed, while simultaneously, a fifth guard brought his bat down hard on Jonah's arm. Jonah dropped the knife and let out a grunt. *Broken for sure.* Another convict swung, this time hitting his shoulder. Jonah fell against the bars as the convicts pounced to finish the fight. Jonah kicked wildly trying to keep them off, but it was no use. Like a swarm of bees they were on top of him swinging their clubs wildly. Before the final club struck his head, Jonah heard the distant sound of footsteps coming down the stairs.

CHAPTER 38

Clark huddled with his back against the concrete wall and his legs tucked into his chest. Only his toes extended past his body far enough to barely touch the metal tracks that on any other day would be supporting a 50 ton metro train hurtling down the rail. The metro station shook so hard, he could feel the concrete below him vibrating from the force of the weapon that hit DC. Children cried. Adults screamed. Dust fell from the ceiling onto his head below. Clark ignored it all, and instead of using his hands to shake the dust out of his hair, he gripped his head in his hands and hid.

Clark couldn't believe it. He kept saying to himself this was just a dream, just a dream, but as the ground continued to rumble and dust continued to fall, he knew this was his new reality. Clark finally snapped out from inside himself at the sound of men shouting. It was far away, but the shouts and screams were unmistakable. Someone cried out in pain from falling rock, a man called for someone to help carry a woman, and yet another was searching for his son, calling the name David over and over again. Shouting erupted all around him but one was louder than the rest. "Get farther down the tunnel," he hollered. "The radiation is seeping in!" People responded by pushing and prodding, migrating deeper into the metro tunnel. The scene was surreal, and Clark saw it as if it was happening in slow motion. He couldn't convince his brain to tell his body to move, but he watched in horror from his seated position, wishing he could will himself to give a hand but instead desiring only to pretend this nightmare was simply a dream.

Clark sat in silence while the tunnel erupted with noises around him. Larger rocks fell, explosions echoed in the distance, and people of all ages wailed with fear, dread, and terror. Eventually, the tunnel itself went completely black. Clark thought he heard someone say that the tunnel entrance had caved in, that they were stuck, but he couldn't process any of it. This was simply too much. Clark continued to sit, contemplating his very existence in the darkness of the subway system.

After some time, most of the people fell silent. A few still wandered around checking the walls and talking to people, but most were sitting just like Clark. The desperation of the situation had come upon most of them now. A small boy covered in dust approached Clark and sat down.

"Do you have any water?" the boy asked. Clark ignored him. "Mister, I'm thirsty," he whined.

Clark finally looked up. "Where's your mom?" Clark asked.

"I don't know," the boy responded. He couldn't have been older than six. "Somehow I was running with people in the street." Tears came to his eyes and he covered them with his hands. "I don't know where they are."

Clark didn't know what to do. He certainly wasn't in a position to comfort the boy. If anything, he felt like he needed somebody to comfort him right now. It was apparent in that moment what had happened, and even with the blissful ignorance of childhood, Clark suspected the boy's tears suggested that the kid had run away from his parents during the initial alarms. What was worse, it was likely the parents had died looking for their son rather than running towards the shelter. With tears streaming down the boy's face, Clark simply put his arm around the boy's shoulder. "We'll find them." He lied.

"When it's not dark anymore?" The child asked.

"Yeah, when it gets light again."

CHAPTER 39

He looked at Evie and she nodded, granting her approval. Jonah flicked the dark green safety cover on the detonator to reveal a silver switch. Along the road, a man wheeled a donkey cart towards them. Sweat dripped down her neck and into her shirt. Africa was so stinking hot. In her hands, she carried a rifle. Jonah looked at her one more time — just to make sure she was ready for what came next. She smiled and nodded again. Jonah moved his thumb in a circular pattern around the switch. One more second. Just a little closer. The donkey cart obliged. The flip of the switch connected a circuit and instantly sent a jolt of electricity to a blasting cap nested firmly within a block of C4. On the other side of the C4 were hundreds of steel balls begging to be released into the target beyond. And they were. Evie stood up as soon as the claymore went off and started firing.

"Get back down!" Jonah shouted. But she wasn't listening and it was too late

anyways. Blood from the donkey soaked her clothes and covered her face. She looked down and smiled. Pure white teeth glowed through the blood and dirt.

"It's time to wake up," he thought he heard her say.

Back in jail. The ground was cold. His head throbbed. Jonah strained to see. He moved his head to the left, and then right. The small figure of a girl came into focus. Her face was dark, but he was certain it was her. So they hadn't killed him. In the small cell, she huddled as far away from him as possible, not sure whether to trust him or fear him. This was the theme of Jonah's life these days: jail and distrust.

He could hear a sound behind him. The rough sound of dragging; clothes pulling against gravel. Jonah moved his head back to the left. Someone was dragging a body up the stairs. *How many had he gotten?* He couldn't remember. Jonah felt for his arm. It didn't hurt as badly as it had. Broken bones healed quickly for him and this was no exception. Aside from the retirement pay, this was the only perk of his military service. Struggling to sit, Jonah positioned himself against the rocks next to the girl.

"I'm here to rescue you." He said flatly, loud enough for whoever was outside those bars to hear fully his intent.

Immediately, laughter filled the cell block. Jonah looked up to see a handful of men standing outside the bars of his cell. In front of them was a smallish man sitting on the stool. His arms were crossed and unlike the others, he didn't appear to find anything funny. Using his foot, the seated man moved the lantern closer. Light danced back and forth, casting his shadow against the far wall. The light also revealed a horrifically scarred face covered in gashes and sores. His hair was long, but thin, and in some places missing all together. It more sprouted than grew and looked ghastly pale.

The laughter trickled off as the man in the center remained silent. Finally, he rose from his stool and approached the bars to the prison.

"You're the prisoner that landed yesterday, aren't you?" he finally asked. Jonah looked at him but didn't respond, so he continued. "You've killed seven of my men in 24 hours. I should probably have you executed." He paused. Jonah remained silent. "I will chalk it up to ignorance. What do you think about that?"

Jonah still wasn't quite sure how to read the situation. The fact that he was still alive and now found himself with a tiny warlord offering to forgive him was an interesting twist. Of course there was an angle, but he couldn't figure it out yet. He saw the men behind the shabby haired warlord exchange looks. They were getting impatient. The sound of a grunt and a strain interrupted them from the stairway. Most of the men looked over to one of the convicts dragging a body up the stairs. Something on the body's belt had gotten caught in a groove in the rocks. Strain as he might, the body wouldn't come loose. Cursing under his breath, the convict bent down to inspect the problem.

The speaker refused to be bothered by his idiot subordinate and continued. "You were wearing orange when you got off that ship. That makes you one of us – regardless of what the other camp may have told you about me. Why don't you tell me your name?"

This was something he was comfortable answering. *Name and rank.* "Jonah," he replied. But he couldn't help himself from continuing "And it was no mistake that I killed your men. They attacked me."

"They were fools and deserved to die," he snapped. "And don't believe what you've been told. My name is Malek, and I rule this camp. I can give you your freedom."

So that was it. He was a convict and was being recruited into this thug's army. His arm was feeling much better and so was his head. Jonah remembered sitting across the table from a Sudanese warlord. The roles were reversed but nonetheless similar. No one in a position of absolute power negotiates with someone that doesn't possess any power of his own. They needed something from the warlord. There were places they couldn't go, things they couldn't do. They needed a friend in the Sudan, and despite the overbearing military might that Jonah had brought with him, he remained powerless to affect the people of that area. That's where the warlord came in. Now that the roles were reversed, Jonah couldn't help but wonder if Malek was in a similar position. Looking for an ally. Smiling to himself, Jonah judged he had a degree of power in the current situation.

"I suppose in exchange for my freedom you want me to do something?" he asked, rising up and moving towards the bars, halting as he reached Malek. At 6 feet, 3 inches tall he towered above him.

"I can give you more than freedom," Malek hissed, taking a

step back from the bars. "I can shower you with delicacies and give you an army to command. All you would have to do is honor me." He paused and then continued. "I can tell you're different, but you're still a killer. You're just like us Jonah, but don't let your past define your future. I could make you rich here on Mars."

Jonah leaned forward pressing against the cage bars. "You never told me what I have to do for my freedom."

Malek turned around and picked the bowie knife up from the ground. Blood still dripped from its blade. He tossed the knife towards the bars and they made a loud clank on impact. "Kill the girl you were sent here to save."

"No." Jonah said flatly.

"We'll execute you both in the morning if her body isn't cold and dead on this cavern floor." Looking at the girl, he scowled, "I think you know how we execute people. I'll let you fill him in. Let's go!" he shouted to his entourage.

With that, Malek stormed up the carved steps and pushed his way past the man still struggling to drag the trapped body to its final resting place. His train followed close on his heels. One man paused, and with weary eyes, dark hair, and a thick brow, he looked at Jonah, and then continued up the stairs to catch up with the others.

<h1 style="text-align:center">CHAPTER 40</h1>

By the time sirens filled the air in Richmond, Virginia, Evie and the children were already in Governor Wilkes' convoy headed west on I-64 towards Lexington, Virginia. The governor was on the phone coordinating for the staging of emergency nuclear response units and getting updates on the establishment of evacuation camps for refugees escaping the blast zone.

Despite having met with Evie in the middle of the night, the Governor and his wife both looked fresh and well dressed. Had she simply caught a glimpse of the man without an understanding of the circumstances surrounding their current movement she would have supposed they were on a political tour rather than escaping a nuclear attack. Evie knew the governor to be a kind and compassionate man, but his face remained stoic, refusing to allow the current circumstances, however dire, to prevent him from focusing on the big picture. Evie couldn't begin to fathom what the bigger picture was, all her motivation was derived from one uninterruptable dream: bring Jonah home. She knew the governor dreamed much bigger however, and even in these circumstances, he was seeing the future for what it should be, not as it currently was.

Mrs. Wilkes, however, was not as good at masking her emotions. Her happy pink dress with clean white leggings and pink heels stood in sharp contrast to the dread showing in her expression. Worry coated her face as she looked out the window of the town car hurtling down I-64. Everyone in the car knew the situation, but nobody would say it. Everything was about to change.

"Oh, God," the governor could be heard saying into his cell phone. "Do they know where?" After a moment longer he continued. "We have to remain on high alert. Call our allies. Has anyone heard from the President? No? His staff? Very well, then. I'll call you from our offices in Lexington." The governor let out a deep sigh as he hung up the phone. Evie examined his face but still couldn't sense any worry.

"Well?" his wife said at last.

"Nuclear missiles hit DC and Los Angeles. Shooting them from inside our own country made them impossible to intercept. Beijing intercepted the final missile and counter-fired." He paused and Mrs. Wilkes gasped. "Not on us… on the Russians. The Russians managed to intercept one, but a second missile hit Samara." The governor paused again and bit his lip. It seemed that verbalizing the events caused their reality to smack him square in the face. His voice quivered as he spoke the next words. "The whole world is at war. I don't know what will happen next."

Evie was somehow less affected than the others in the car. She wrapped her arms around her daughter, Eden, and patted Titus on the shoulder. Nathan sat contently staring out the window in his car seat. She envied him in a way. Whatever the world became would all be normal for him. He wouldn't know any different. Her world had been turned upside down nearly a year ago. There was nothing left on this earth that could affect her as long as her children remained safe and healthy. They were headed to the mountains, but not even nuclear war could change what she fought for. She would still fight to bring Jonah home, and only then would her already shattered world begin to mend itself. "Why did the Chinese attack the Russians?" she asked at last, breaking the silence in the black town car currently being escorted through Charlottesville, Virginia.

At first the governor didn't respond. He was quietly watching the sun rise over the campus at the University of Virginia. Their car was at such an angle to the large red brick building that the sun seemed to weave its way through the massive white columns of the covered walkway. At last, he broke his gaze and turned his attention to Evie. "We believe the Russians were responsible for the attack. I don't think they expected the Chinese to figure it out so quickly."

"And the President?" Evie asked, wondering how D.C. fared.

"Nobody has heard anything from the White House, but it's not entirely out of character. This president keeps everything tight and under wraps. If I didn't know better, I'd suspect he intended to blame this on us." John looked at his wife. "I hate myself for even considering this, Ruth." He paused, looked around the car and at Evie and the kids, and then continued. "Whatever damage is done, is done. Maybe this will be the event that can unite the nation under common ideals. And maybe, just maybe, the president is no longer here to create divisions." John Wilkes tapped on the window, and his driver lowered it on command. "Aaron, when we get to Lexington I want to make a statement to the press. Please make the necessary coordination for security."

John turned his attention back to the car window and appeared to sink deeply into thought. Eden looked up at Evie and smiled.

"Do you remember when daddy tried to fix the toilet and toilet water shot in his face?" She startled giggling, and Titus laughed even harder. Nathan, still stuck in his car seat, looked back and forth at them before joining in with laughter, his fat cheeks bouncing as he chortled. The governor remained stoic with his eyes fixed on the window, but Mrs. Wilkes smiled.

"Wasn't that gross?" Evie replied, scrunching her nose and touching it to Eden's. Eden giggled louder and declared "he got poop water all over his face!"

With that, even Mrs. Wilkes started to laugh and the boys laughed louder still. Evie hadn't thought about that for a long time. Jonah had come down soaked. Of course it wasn't soiled water, it was just clean water from the copper tips, but it was hilarious all the same. He shouted for towels and marched the two oldest, wearing rubber gloves and rain boots, up to the bathroom to help him clean up. Evie smiled at the memory. She desperately hoped Jonah was faring better than Earth was.

CHAPTER 41

Jonah reached through the bars of his prison cell to pick up the knife. Candle light from the lantern glistened off the blade as he slipped it back through the bars and placed it in his belt.

"Please don't kill me," the girl whimpered.

"I'm not going to kill you," he replied, distractedly, looking around the cell. "We're going to get out of here before the lights come on."

The girl wrapped her arms around her knees and pulled them tightly to her chest. Jonah moved around the cell checking the ceiling for gaps and inspecting the bars for points of weakness. He found none. The cell appeared to be impenetrable.

"I guess it doesn't matter," she murmured. "It's probably better to be crushed by a giant rock then go back to the camp."

Jonah paused. "What's wrong with going back to the camp?"

"I don't know… people disappear there. And there are noises at night."

Jonah kneeled down in front of her. As he bent down close to her, he could see the cuts and burns on her arms and legs. Some of gashes looked like bite marks on her forearms. Gently, he put his hand on her arm. "What's your name?"

"I saw you kill those people." She responded. "I've never seen anyone do what you did."

Jonah looked down at the ground and climbed back up to his feet.

"My name's Adiela – people call me Adi" she said.

"Well, Adi, we're going to get out of here and I'm going to get you back to your parents."

"I don't have any parents," Adiela responded, still curled up against the cavern wall.

"Where are they?"

"They just disappeared. I don't know. Lots of people disappear. I don't know where…" She trailed off and then paused. "They were miners. We came here to mine because my dad couldn't get a job on Earth. They've been missing for months now."

Jonah was perplexed. Her story sounded just like Zoe's. *Why would the mining company continue sending people to Mars if the mining operations had stopped? Why would the government send him to a prison on*

Mars if they hadn't spoken to their guards in years? Did they know what had happened here? How could they not? But if they didn't know, surely they thought something was wrong. Where did the marines go? Don't they have to report to someone on Earth? Nothing fit, but he was convinced he knew who had the answers.

"What do you know about the noises that I've been hearing?" Jonah asked.

The glimmer of light from a lantern descending the steps interrupted their conversation. It was a face he had seen before, the one who paused after his meeting with Malek. Behind him he drug a body. The man moaned. He was still alive. Reaching the bottom of the steps, the man rolled the half conscious body to the bars. A set of keys was attached to the body's waist.

"We don't have much time, so listen and do what I say," The man commanded firmly in a thick German accent. "We're done with Malek. He's cruel and has no foresight. He doesn't have what we need to make it here long term. Get the girl to safety, and meet me in the farms below this fissure tomorrow. We can help each other."

Not willing to wait for a response, the man turned and quickly ascended the stairwell. On the ground against the bars, the wounded convict moaned and tried to climb to his knees. Jonah snatched his collar and pulled him close to the bars.

Taking the knife from his belt, he looked at Adiela. "You won't want to watch this, Adi."

CHAPTER 42

Charlie Miller prepared to board a plane from beautiful Washington State to Roanoke, Virginia where he and his company would provide security to a man named John Wilkes, the Governor of Virginia. It was amazing how quickly the investigation into their airfield incursion was tabled in the face of this new disaster, but while on any other day, a dropped investigation would bring hope, Charlie only felt fear as to what was coming next.

After an hour on the airfield neither the president, the vice president, the secretary of defense, nor the members of his cabinet could be contacted. Following several attempts, General Parker, the three star commanding general at Fort Hood, declared a national state of emergency and told the press he was assuming power over the nation until an interim government could be established. General Parker's command deployed the regiment to protect key leaders in the nation's government while conventional forces were deployed to secure additional strategic sites and lock down the nation's borders. National Guard and Reserve forces were deployed to assist police in keeping order and aid in the decontamination and recovery effort of both D.C. and Los Angeles.

As he ascended the steps of the Boeing 747, Charlie found himself uncontrollably drawn back into the past. Charlie didn't consider himself sentimental, but he still closed his eyes and ran his hands along the cold metallic rails leading into the passenger cabin. Every deployment, as he ascended the steps of potentially the last plane he would fly in, Charlie Miller held the rail and forced himself to remember that last moment. The cold metallic cylinder pressing against his hands reminded him of what he was leaving and the austere conditions he would soon find himself in. While he placed little value on his one bedroom apartment, and had become accustomed to leaving his bed for a cot somewhere, this time felt different and he sensed he might never return. Drops of rain splattered on the narrow stairway as Charlie climbed into the plane, as if heaven itself was mourning the catastrophe unfolding before him.

At last, Charlie reached the top of the steps and was greeted by a flight attendant who was far too young to have such a serious expression on her face. As the last person to load the plane, Charlie stopped in front of her. "We're going to get through this." he tried to assure her.

"My family was living in D.C." she said. Even the action of uttering those words was too much for her, as if finally saying it led her to the reality she had previously refused to accept: that she no longer had a family. Tears formed and then dripped down her red cheeks as insistently as the downpour outside their white Boeing 747. Before Charlie could respond, a second flight attendant took her by the shoulders and led her deeper into the cabin. Charlie found his seat.

CHAPTER 43

The sun rising over Mars was encircled by a blue haze as its rays reflected off the dust and gas in the atmosphere. The sun looked comically small as it rose above the two ridges that walled their hotel inside a protected valley. Zoe wished she had paid more attention to the company's promotional videos about where they were located.

As Zoe looked out the large glass hotel window, her stomach twisted and wrenched. She hoped that she'd have woken up to the smell of her mom cooking bacon on the stove and the sound of cars honking on a busy New Jersey highway. She'd stroll down the hallway to hear her father fussing over something in the newspaper, or maybe he'd even be clicking on the computer going through job after job after job and explaining to her mom why they wouldn't hire him so it would be no use applying. Instead, Zoe went to bed alone and woke up alone. Nobody cooked breakfast or doted over her. The TV wasn't on. No parents were arguing. Her nightmare was not over. In fact, it wasn't even a nightmare because a nightmare meant that this was a dream. This wasn't a dream. This was now her life.

Zoe climbed back onto her bed and buried her head in the pillows. She wanted to cry again but couldn't. There weren't any more tears left and her jaw hurt desperately from clenching her teeth. As she remembered the events from the last few days, there was a knock on her door.

"Zoe," called a familiar voice. It was Jillian. "Zoe."

Zoe jumped from the bed, relieved to have a person take her thoughts off the past. As she opened the door, a red-faced Jillian pushed her way through and immediately started ordering her about.

"Zoe, you aren't dressed yet? There's a clean jumpsuit in the closet. But get in the shower first. Let's go Zoe, there's lots to do today."

Zoe rubbed her eyes, walked into the bathroom, and closed the door behind her.

"I'll be in the lobby!" Jillian called as Zoe turned the water on.

Showered and changed, Zoe descended the stairs into the lobby. The lobby looked frozen in time, completely unchanged from the scene they had observed when they first arrived. The same characters sat in chairs reading and chatting while another crew was at the bar. The bartender looked flat and uninvolved as she poured drinks for her patrons.

Jillian, seated on a bench in the lobby, jumped up when she saw Zoe, and hurried over.

"Oh Zoe, you look so much better," Jillian fussed. "And I'll bet you feel better too, don't you?"

Zoe nodded and attempted a smile while Jillian continued, not giving her a chance to speak.

"Well! We've got a lot to do today. Whenever someone joins our group we have to take them to the clinic. They'll do a few tests on you to make sure that you don't pose any risk to the group. We'll also want to verify your blood type and medical history."

"I already did all those tests before we came out here, though," Zoe protested, resisting Jillian's pull on her arm to get moving in that direction.

"Oh, Zoe, they don't check for the same things we do here. We've learned a lot in the years we've been running this colony. The things you don't think are important suddenly become more important than you can imagine."

Before Zoe could react, she was being pulled down the hallway by a breathless Jillian Jaspers, swishing and swooshing her pants all the way into a clinic and onto a bed.

"Just lay here. I'll be back with our doctor." Jillian said as she closed the door leaving Zoe alone.

Zoe sat up and looked around. The room was cold and the florescent lights reflected brightly off plain white walls. While in typical clinics posters showing the skeletal and nervous system decorated the room, this place remained bare. By the time the doctor arrived to inspect Zoe, she already had goose bumps on her arms and legs.

The elderly man had hair as white as the room around him. He wore dark slacks, a stained lab coat, and carried a rusty clipboard under his left arm. He didn't come in smiling or with much gusto, but he looked kind and when he shook her hand it was warm and fatherly.

"Well, Zoe," he started, looking down at his paper, "it is very nice to finally meet you. I've been looking through your charts ever since they were sent from Earth, and, Zoe, I must be honest, you look very promising." Looking up at Zoe, he smiled, revealing a row of perfect teeth and then dove into his inspection. He felt her ankles and knees and moved her elbows to and fro. He had her rotate her head and focus on his finger as he moved it side to side. She bent over, touched her toes, and he felt her spine. He took her pulse, listened to her breathing, and took her temperature.

"You're in perfect health," he finally proclaimed after writing some notes down on his clipboard. "We're just going to draw a little bit of blood and run some compatibility tests. Then you're all set. Would you just lean back for me?"

Zoe leaned back and took a deep breath, felt the rubber band synch tightly around her bicep, and then the sharp prick of a needle. She squinted as he began to draw blood and when he jostled the needle releasing the rubber band, she grimaced.

"You're all set." He proclaimed, removing it from her arm and placing a cotton swab and band aid in its place. "You can head back to your room now; Ms. Jaspers will get you when we have the results." Zoe was led out the door and passed a stone-faced Jillian in the hallway on her way back to her room. As she looked back she could see the two talking in the hallway.

"What do you think?"

"She's healthy. They picked us a good one. We'll have to see if her white blood cells attack the host. I'll let you know before tomorrow morning."

CHAPTER 44

Evie Shepherd woke up just in time to watch the exit for I-64 zip by their motorcade and the town of Lexington, Virginia zip by with it. John had just set down his phone and was once again gazing thoughtfully out of the town car's rear passenger window.

"I thought we were headed to Lexington," Evie asked the Governor.

"We're going to Roanoke now." He replied, exchanging a quick glance with her before returning to the window.

Roanoke? What could possibly be in Roanoke, Evie wondered. Looking around, she was glad to see her children still sleeping. The early morning made the rest of the car trip bearable. Evie wanted to know more from the governor but she didn't want to bother him. His gaze out of the limo across the majestic Blue Ridge mountain range that shadowed I-81 was steady and unreadable. Evie knew that John Wilkes was analyzing the day ahead of him over and over again in his head.

Evie looked towards his wife who had fixed her gaze on her youngest, Nathan. Noticing the stare, Mrs. Wilkes looked up to Evie and smiled warmly. Her eyes were moist but no tears ran down her face.

"I was just wondering what this little one's life was going to be like," she said, moving her shoulder length blond hair to behind her ear. "There has been so much change in the world today."

Evie didn't respond. She didn't know how. There was too much change in this little boy's life. And what would the future hold? Without a father, and now, without a home? Evie was grateful for the Wilkes family, but how much could they truly do? *Was his future doomed to a life of violence and combat, just like his father? Would surviving mean to be sucked forever into poverty and war?*

"I'm sorry, I didn't mean to suggest that his outlook was gloom." Mrs. Wilkes said, interrupting Evie's thoughts. "I'm sure this generation will prevail as we always have."

It was Evie now whose eyes were moist. She looked at the other two children and felt panic. Her face felt hot. Nausea bubbled up from her stomach and battled for control of her throat. *How could Evie possibly provide a real future for these three without Jonah?* Everything she had done up to this point was for Jonah; her children had always been safe. But now she had to consider their children. She couldn't petition for him anymore. She couldn't even bear the thought. This was all too much. Her children would be her focus now, and that thought terrified her, not because they were never the focus, but because with Jonah as the focus, he was there near her heart to help her raise them. That wasn't possible anymore. She had to accept reality… and it was too dark for her to see through.

"What's in Roanoke, John?" she suddenly asked, surprised she didn't care about disturbing him any longer.

John shifted his gaze from the mountains to Evie. His eyes were always soft and calming, but she unexpectedly felt as if they lured her as a politician rather than a friend. "We've been assigned a security detachment from the commander of the remnant of our forces. We are going there to pick them up." John stopped as if to end the conversation, but when Evie continued to return his gaze, he gave her the real reason. "The Chinese are sending a delegation to Roanoke. As the senior government official, I am going to be negotiating with them over what to do with Russia."

His answer sent shivers down Evie's neck. The Chinese, the Russians, and the Americans were the only global powers remaining, were staunch competitors, and were currently engaged in nuclear war. Evie felt the need to get out of the car and run in any direction but Roanoke, as if not negotiating would somehow end the conflict all together. Helpless, she remained seated and pondered their future. For the first time in months, Jonah could not have been further from Evie's mind.

CHAPTER 45

As the sun set on the valley, the lights in the tunnels also began to fade. At first they dimmed, but as Mars rotated on its axis and the sun wearily escaped the two ridges that captured its light by day, the lights eventually faded entirely. As the lights went out in the tunnels, the eerie green saliva that coated the tunnel walls began to glow. Jonah couldn't be certain, but they seemed to glow more radiantly tonight than before. As if in collusion with the setting sun, the temperature dropped quickly inside the small alcove where Jonah and Adi waited.

While Jonah was warm in his high performance jump suit, Adi began to shiver as the temperatures fell with the coming night. Her suit had been torn from her during her kidnap and what was left of her garments had been shredded during her torture. Now her clothes were now no more than loosely fitting rags. Adi wrapped her arms around herself and tried to control her chattering teeth as they waited for the austere visitor to deliver his message. As occurred the night prior, carbon dioxide fog seeped through the cavern walls and pooled on the rocky floor of their makeshift hideaway.

They could have escaped all the way to the miner's camp, but Jonah was worried he wouldn't be able to sneak back out to meet with the man with the agenda. He needed to keep the meeting to get information to help him negotiate from a position of power with Jillian Jaspers. At this stage in his journey, Jonah knew the only way to survive was to know everything about everything. Otherwise, he risked being a pawn to someone else's will, or worse off, he risked being dead.

In the thick fog illuminated by green light, Jonah had a jarring thought. It was something that Adi had said in the cell. Something he had forgotten until now. *People disappear.* But it wasn't just anyone. After all, the lobby in the hotel was packed with adults. And if parents disappeared, why did their daughter remain alive? And why did she run off? His chain of thoughts eventually led to its source and his worry. *Zoe.* Parentless, she was completely alone in the hotel. She had no one to look after her.

"Adi," Jonah asked. "What did you mean when you said people disappeared at the miner's camp?"

Adi looked at him for a second and then back down at the

thick pools of carbon dioxide swirling around their feet. She was wondering if she could trust him or if he would believe her. Finally, confirming his second theory, she said "You wouldn't believe me if I told you."

"I think I'd believe anything at this point," Jonah responded faking a smile. "The fact that I'm having a conversation with you in a breathable tunnel on Mars in front of glowing corn or whatever the hell that plant is should be enough for anyone to believe anything."

She smiled at him but continued staring at the ground.

"Adi, why did you run away? What made you think hiding in the farms or being captured by prisoners would be better than the hotel?"

"The scientists at the hotel. I think they are doing experiments on us. When a young person arrives, they don't last long. Didn't you notice there were only adults? There are no young people in the hotel. It's weird. As soon as they show up, they're gone. They usually only stay a few days." The sincerity on her face was clear and her expression inspired him to believe her.

"But what about the bartender? She looked young." Jonah replied, trying to piece together whether she was explaining a real trend or a childish fear.

"She's the one that told me to run. She said they did tests on her, but she wasn't compatible. Her parents are missing too. She hates it there."

"Not compatible?"

"I don't know. That's just what she said. But they did tests on me, too." She paused. "After that, the girl told me to escape if I could."

"Tests? What kind of tests?" Jonah had to know what was going on. Immediately after he asked, he regretted it. Adi's eyes welled up and she pulled her knees even closer to her chest; burying her head in her legs. Fear poured over Jonah. He felt hot. Panicked. *Zoe.* The name came back to him like a spear thrust violently into his chest. Suddenly, there was no time to waste. He sat, hiding from convict patrols, waiting for a stranger to feed him a nonsense story to fulfill a selfish agenda while Zoe waited for him in extreme danger of something. How could he have left her there?!

A beam of light moving towards them interrupted his thoughts. It was faint at first, but the glow became a rich red and orange as the light, and its carrier, entered the farms. The carrier stopped before he reached the first row of crops, pausing in the center of the entryway. Signaling to Adi to be quiet, Jonah climbed gracefully off the cavern ledge that marked their hiding spot. As Jonah approached, the man raised the lantern to his face to blow out the flame, plunging them into the eerie green light of the farms. The plants once again took charge and projected their green hue across the cavern and through the fog. Jonah circumvented the crops counter-clockwise to prevent this mystery man from identifying where he left Adi and approached him from behind.

"Did you turn the lantern off as a signal to others?" Jonah

whispered in his ear.

Spinning around with shock, the treasonous convict stumbled backwards to create some distance between him and Jonah. Jonah closed the distance quickly and snatched him by the collar of his jumpsuit, stepped past him, and with one smooth motion, used his foot to knock him off his feet. Holding the convict inches from the ground he gazed hard into his eyes.

"There's no one else... I swear... it's just me," the man quickly stammered, still shocked by Jonah's strength and speed.

"Why are we here? What do you think we can do for each other?" Jonah demanded.

He had decided he would negotiate aggressively for two reasons. First, he was convinced that if the man had brought others with him, he could potentially spur them into an attack if they thought the man's life was threatened. This could be to Jonah's advantage if they attacked with haste, rather than catching him off-guard from behind. He also assumed the convict was fully aware of what Jonah had done to the other prisoners. His hope was that he could intimidate genuine truth out of the man. His tactic seemed to work, but he couldn't be sure if it worked because the man wanted to tell the truth all along, or if it was because the treasonous convict was scared.

The convict regained his composure and gripped Jonah's forearm to prevent the discomfort of the pressure of his jumpsuit from cutting into his skin. Looking up at Jonah he gave a nervous smile, suggesting he was ready to answer his questions.

"Name's Dieter. I'm one of Malek's generals. Please, let me up and I'll explain. There's no one else with me." Eying him cautiously, Jonah raised Dieter back to his feet. Smoothing out his uniform, Dieter continued, "I know it probably seems there's no one you can trust here, and honestly, it's true. But when we heard what you did when you first landed, we knew you were the answer to our problems."

"What problems? How am I the answer?"

"After the rebellion, after the camps split in two, both sides began working to control the limited resources left here, as well as, determining who would lead them. For the miners it was easy. The scientists clearly had the education and we organized our camp as justly as we could…"

Jonah interrupted. "We?"

"I was a scientist. Only much later did I escape to join the convicts."

"Why?"

"I'm not sure you'd believe me if I told you," Dieter replied.

There was that phrase again. Apparently everyone believed their stories were so absurd, that no outsider would take them seriously. Coming from a child, it made sense. Coming from a man who claimed to be a scientist, however, made it slightly more unnerving. What could be so bad that a scientist would flee into the criminal camp?

"So, this thing I wouldn't believe," Jonah replied. "That's why you left the miner's camp and joined the convicts?"

"I know it sounds strange, but I couldn't contribute to their projects anymore. By the time I offered my services to Malek, he had fully gained control. I admit, he gained control in a far more brutal fashion, but Malek is… uncomplicated. He's controllable… or at least he was."

"What do you mean?" Jonah inquired.

"Malek is simple. His desires are simple. When you know what a man wants, you can remove his ability to think for himself. When his desires are carnal and when his disposition is lazy, you can control him because you can control his experience. You give him what he wants and you solve his problems before he realizes he has any. Before he knows it, he's not sure what he would do without you, and, that is power."

Jonah was intrigued; this appeared to be a man of considerable intelligence, but that meant he was considerably more dangerous, too. Despite the brutality he imagined the man had worked on Malek's behalf, he found himself believing his story. Maybe it was because he desperately wanted to believe there was a man with just one iota of honesty on this planet. Maybe he was desperate. But there was something else too. His mannerisms went against every convict he had thus far interacted with: crude, brutal, and ignorant. Dieter was none of these things; rather, he appeared calm, collected, thoughtful, and intelligent.

"Unfortunately," the man continued, "Malek's taste for power was more vicious than any of us wanted, and soon he added paranoia to his montage of attributes."

"So this is where you ask me to do something for you; and in exchange I suppose you grant me what the miners and Malek offered as well?"

Dieter shrugged as if Jonah didn't actually have a choice. "Jonah, do you remember the miner talking to one of our scouts when you first landed?"

"Yes," he responded, suspicious. He did remember; he remembered every detail and desperately wondered what they had been saying.

"Aren't you curious what they said to each other?" Dieter paused, giving Jonah a calculated glance, and then continued without providing Jonah the opportunity to speak. "What am I saying; of course you are. The miner told my scout they were sending you to us tonight. They wanted you dead and out of their way. In fact, if Malek had his way, you would be."

Jonah was listening, but when he realized the totality of what Dieter had been telling him he felt his world caving in – again. He had abandoned Zoe without fully understanding the situation. He knew without a doubt that she was in danger. He had to go back to get her.

Dieter could tell Jonah was distressed but misattributed his distress for self-preservation. "Doesn't feel good to know you were lied to and sent to your death, does it?"

"The girl I was with, the young girl, when I landed. Is she in danger?" he asked hastily.

"You have no idea..." Dieter trailed off, but seeing the shock on Jonah's face he quickly continued. "I'm sure they made us sound evil; but we kidnapped young women from the miners because of what they were doing to them. It was Malek that made the decision to do awful things to them here... that's not what the rest of us wanted."

"Then why did you continue to take them?" Jonah asked; anger rising inside of him.

"Because what Malek does to them is infinitely better than the fate they face with Jillian."

CHAPTER 46

The urgency that coursed through Jonah was overwhelming. No longer in mental control of his own body, he raced down the roughly 5 miles of tunnel that connected the convict's camp to the Hotel Olympia. Despite the thinner Martian air and the carbon dioxide seeping through the red cavern walls, his lungs refused to surrender. Each time he even considered slowing to a walk, a fresh surge of fear and adrenaline rushed through his veins.

His mind was split along two lines of thought and constantly danced back and forth between the worst case scenarios for each. In one stream, Zoe was being subjected to a horrific scientific experiment and he would arrive too late to save her; in the other, she was relaxing on her bed and everything was just a big misunderstanding. . His lungs burned for oxygen, his throat throbbed, and his heart pounded. But there was no time and his panic was also tied to Adi. He had trusted Dieter to look after her but still couldn't be certain of his motives. He couldn't bear to consider what she would be subjected to if he was wrong about Dieter, the intelligent self-seeking traitor. Someone was lying - and Jonah was the one that stood to lose something.

Hope is what continued to drive Jonah onward. The faster he ran, the more he allowed himself to hope. His heart thudded inside his chest; but he would not give it reprieve. Jonah would not be defeated. But one question still rang in his mind. *Could he save them both?*

****

Zoe rubbed her eyes as Jillian led her down the familiar lobby staircase, through the throngs of miners, and towards the clinic. According to Jillian, they had found something in her blood test that had to be addressed and couldn't wait for morning. It was dire, she had claimed, and could put the whole colony in jeopardy.

Zoe certainly didn't want to be the cause of a sickness or plague spreading through the colony she now called her home. If there was something Jillian could do, she was happy to oblige; and how could it not be serious. After all, they woke her up at two a.m. Despite the time of night, the lobby hummed with the same crowd. Some had fallen asleep in their chairs while others waited at the bar chatting. On Mars, regardless of where the sun was, day and night were simply words. Without any purpose, the guests of Hotel Olympia napped when they chose, visited when they wanted to, and did their best to drown their memories with alcohol. Lots of alcohol. Zoe suspected many of them desired to drown more than their memories.

No one acknowledged the tired girl being led by Jillian except the young woman tending to her customers from behind the bar. They locked eyes only for a moment, but in that time, all Zoe saw was fear; the kind of ice cold fear that sent panic rippling through her extremities in a way she could never have described. Zoe froze. Terrified to go onward but unable to stop walking. The grip of Jillian's hands didn't loosen, but tightened, and soon Zoe felt as if she was powerless to Jillian's momentum, dragging her down the long hallway towards the clinic.

****

By the time Jonah saw the light of the miner's checkpoint he was beyond exhaustion. His lungs craved oxygen that wasn't available. Slowing to a walk, he tried to regain his composure, worried he would not be able to lift his arms to fight if he was confronted. The men's reaction to him was typical. While startled at first, they were unconcerned about letting him pass. This should have been a reassurance that everything was okay, but instead it worried Jonah even more. *Could they really have no idea? How could they be so ignorant?*

Jonah wheezed as he crossed through the barriers but forced his body to jog as he made his way up the long stairwell that fed into the hotel lobby.

With the bar finally closed, the entryway was void of patrons. The girl tending the bar was cleaning the metallic surface and paid him no attention as he entered. Jonah felt his strength return on the last stretch of this nightmarish trek and bolted up the stairs, taking them two at a time. Finally, reaching Zoe's room he pounded ferociously at the door. No answer. Jonah pounded again, this time even harder, but all he heard was silence. Any hope that Jonah had fled him and was instantly replaced by fear. Not just fear. Dread. Every muscle, ligament, tendon, and joint ached with dread. He leaned back putting as much force into his leg as possible to kick the door in. Flying off the hinges, the door gave way exposing what he most feared. An empty room.

****

Zoe had been told to undress and climb into a white hospital gown. After she was covered, two large men came in with Jillian and asked her to lie back on the cold sterile hospital bed. Examining it for the first time, she noticed arms with leather straps.

"What do you need to do to me? What do I have that's so dangerous?" Zoe asked, almost pleading, desperately trying to avoid climbing onto the bed. In her gut, she knew this wasn't right. Something was wrong. Terribly wrong. The instincts Zoe had to flee, however, were leveled by the reality that she had nowhere to go. Quiet defiance was not a weapon, but all she could hope to muster.

Jillian didn't answer. Instead the two men that escorted Jillian into the room lifted Zoe off her feet, thrust her onto the bed, and strapped her arms down. Flailing was useless. She was no match against two full grown men.

"Please," she pleaded after the men stepped back behind Jillian. "Please tell me what you're going to do. I'm not fighting, I just want to know."

Jillian stepped to the side of the table making space for the kindly doctor that inspected her the first time to step forward.

"Zoe," he said smiling. "We requested you from Earth because of your miraculous test results. But we needed to do one more blood test just to be certain."

He was insane. Smiling wildly, his row of white teeth now looked to be a stained yellow. A hideous yellow. Behind his glasses, Zoe saw eyes that were as dark and soulless as the tunnels of Mars itself. What she'd mistaken for a kindly family doctor was a mad scientist as evil as Dr. Frankenstein.

"Your blood," he continued, "demonstrated a remarkable ability to coexist with a specific microbe. Your antibodies completely ignore it." He took a deep breath in and looked at Jillian as if to say, we've done it. "Zoe, do you know what your name means?"

Zoe simply stared in shock. Time slowed as she realized how

insane these two were. "It means life, Zoe. Life!" He grew more and more excited as he spoke. "Please know we've restrained you for your own good. If you fully grasped the opportunity we were putting before you, if you truly understood, you'd have volunteered readily."

Jillian, who had remained silent, spoke up. "Zoe, you are the answer to all of our searching, and with the tiny prick of this needle, you'll do more for Mars than you could ever imagine. *You* will be the start of sustainable life on Mars, the mother of all the living!"

Trying to comprehend what she had said, Zoe sunk back into the depths of her mind. Watching almost in a detached state as the "doctor" revealed a syringe the length of his hand. Time not only slowed, but now became more distant. Soon, Zoe felt as if she was watching herself as an outside observer. She not only felt the cold perspiration dripping down her cheeks, but could see it. As the Dr. Frankenstein approached, the needle appeared. In astonishment she watched as it grew to be not just the size of his hand, but appeared to be the size of his entire arm.

****

Flying down the stairs and into the lobby Jonah turned left to search Jillian's office for any clues of the girl.

"She went the other way, to the clinic!" shouted the bartender, now completely in tune to what was going on.

"How long ago?" Jonah shouted back as he twisted his body to turn the other way.

"About an hour; you don't have much time!"

Jonah raced down the hallway to the clinic. The lights were out in the waiting room, but a small crack of florescent light emanated from a partially closed door. Not knowing what to expect, Jonah approached the door slowly and deliberately. Peering through the crack, he could see four people in the room including Jillian. The door obscured his view from the remainder of the room, hiding the figure on the bed.

Reckless with concern, Jonah took a deep breath and thrust the door open, surprising those inside. Shocked, the two larger men took a step towards him but were halted by Jillian's voice. The doctor was standing by the sink holding a needle.

"Where's Zoe?" he demanded.

"Jonah, you're alive!? You made it?! What about the girl. Did you rescue her?"

"Where's Zoe," he shouted again.

The two men parted and lying on the bed was an unconscious Zoe, dressed in a hospital robe with her arms strapped to the rails.

Jonah rushed through the door to unstrap her, but once again the sight of the bed closed by the bodies of the oversized miners blocking its path. From their belts, they removed cattle prods.

"What did you do to her?" he shouted at Jillian, and then looking at the doctor, repeated himself.

"Oh Jonah," Jillian responded. "Don't be so naïve. Do you think, after all that you've seen, that we have any choice here? Look around you! Mars is in chaos. Earth is yet again on the verge of war. We are doing everything we can, but progress requires sacrifice. You of all people know that, don't you Jonah?"

"I'm taking her. Get out of my way."

"That's not advisable," Jillian shrugged. "If she was to have symptoms, or her body was to reject the procedure…well, she would experience a lot of pain. You can't help her now; she's ours, Jonah."

It was clear that Jillian thought she was right. Righteous, even. The savior of mankind. She was basking in her own self-proclaimed power. And while she was clearly insane, she held all the cards. She had two of the biggest miners he had ever seen holding cattle prods, the doctor had just injected Zoe with something horrible, and they were the only medical facility on this planet. Jonah had to level the playing field, and he knew just what to do.

Eying the cart to his left, Jonah stepped inside the door, moved in front of the cart and kicked it as hard as he could towards the two men. Catching them off-guard, it smashed into the knees of the first, causing him to stagger backwards. The second jumped out of the way, but one on one, he was no match for Jonah's strength and speed. The man swung with his electric cattle prod. Jonah dodged to his outside, grabbed his fully extended arm and snapped his elbow down hard on his own knee. The man screamed and dropped the electrified prod into Jonah's waiting hand. Just as he had intended. Before the second guard could recover, Jonah stuck the electric prod to his throat and pressed the switch. The man fell to his knees and began to vomit uncontrollably.

In the chaos, Jillian rushed through the door before he could stop her, the doctor close on her heals. Jonah barely managed to grab the white jacket, cutting off the doctor's escape. "What'd you do to her, you psycho?" Jonah shouted at him, still high off the adrenaline from the fight.

Jonah backed the doctor against the wall. "It was just a sedative, I swear."

"Liar!" Jonah accused. "I spoke with Dieter. I know about your experiments. Now, what did you do to her?" Jonah raised the cattle prod aggressively with his free hand, but instead, turned and used it to put the miner back down on his belly. The doctor used his hands to cover his face and glared at him through the cracks in his fingers while relaying a solemn warning.

"How many people do you think you can take? I suggest you leave before Jillian comes back with more."

Wanting to exact revenge, but knowing the truth of what the insane doctor was saying, Jonah unclasped the leather straps that restrained Zoe and carried her out the door and away from the clinic.

CHAPTER 47

Having successfully brought Adiela back into his living quarters, Dieter, or Doc Deet as the convicts called him, began to inspect the girl's wounds and apply the appropriate dressings. He had her wrapped in a large army green wool blanket and gently encouraged her to eat soup he had heated from last night's dinner.

To call Doc Deet one of Malek's generals was certainly an overstatement. He had never led anyone, and no convicts had been assigned to him. He was, after all, a scientist. More specifically he was a psychologist and, right up until the chaos on Mars ensued, he was quite a successful one. While Malek preferred to refer to him as one of his eight generals, many of them actually weren't generals of any army at all. In fact, they were much more like cabinet members, offering advice and assisting him in running the day-to-day activities of his operation.

What Doc Deet offered, however, was far more than psychology. He had seen the inner workings of the miner's camp. He had participated in the experiments. He was trained to perform maintenance on machinery. But while Malek liked his skills, he cared much more for his mind. To Malek, the difference between a psychologist and a psychic was moot. To him, they were the same, and because of this, Malek used him to read people's motives. And, without realizing it, he had also singlehandedly given Dieter all the power.

As Dieter moved from cut to cut, Adi cringed and occasionally flinched from the sharp sting of the home-made alcohol solution he pressed against her wounds. In his assessment, none of them needed stitches, which was good because he didn't know how to close a wound and wasn't sure he could do so without fainting. Dabbing alcohol and applying salve and bandages was the extent of his medical skills.

"You know," he told Adi, "we've been waiting for a man like Jonah to come around for a long time." Adi didn't say anything but appeared interested, so he continued. "I know I could never lead, but we can't let that madman rule forever. It's time for change. Time for us to live in harmony with one another. Time to make the best of the situation and do something good here."

"Jillian won't let you," Adiela finally replied.

Dieter looked up at her and grinned. "That's the beauty of it.

When we unite under Jonah, she won't have a choice."

His thick German accent made him sound utterly evil, but his calm demeanor and the patience with which he cleaned Adiela's injuries made her think. *Jonah running things on Mars.* In the short few hours she had spent with him, he had done miraculous things. *Maybe he could make this a life worth living,* she thought.

After cleaning her cuts, Dieter settled her down on his couch, covering her in the green wool blanket. This was Adiela's first look at how the other side lived. The *evil* camp that Jillian Jaspers had repeatedly warned them about. After their escape from the prison below, the convicts had occupied the marine barracks. Malek had apparently reserved the officers' quarters for his most trusted companions.

Compared to the red colored rock and iron clad dungeon she had become accustomed to, the marine barracks were clean and comfortable. Dieter's was a three room apartment complete with a kitchen, living room, bathroom, and bedroom. The living room that she slept in had large windows that overlooked one of the western valleys. It was a picturesque scene and for the first time, despite all the uncertainty, Adiela saw a degree of beauty on Mars.

Adi hadn't noticed they'd ascended above the surface, but was happy to see the dark Martian landscape that rolled out before her like an unmade bed. A dust storm must have rolled into their camp over the last few days because dry lightning lit up the sky. Extravagant bolts of red and white beat the heavens ferociously and exposed deep crevices along the deserted terrain. Sinking into the couch, Adi pulled her blanket up over her eyes and searched for sleep. As she drifted off, she let her mind wander back to Jonah. *Had he been successful in rescuing the girl?* Smiling to herself, she allowed herself to hope that maybe he would rescue them all.

CHAPTER 48

Jonah raced left and navigated down the long hallway. Trying as he might to sprint, all he could manage was an awkward hobble with unconscious Zoe slung over his shoulders. His heart, heavy with exhaustion, refused to allow Jonah to consider pushing himself any faster. Clearly, his weekly bike rides with the kids followed by sleeping for five months had not done enough to prepare him for his latest trial. Reaching an intersection, Jonah turned right leading to another hallway. He had no idea where he was going, but was certain he couldn't go back the way he had come. The doctor was right – Jillian and whatever evil she was planning would not allow Jonah or Zoe to escape. She was most certainly rousing everyone she could find.

Closed doors lined the hallway that Jonah now found himself in. His shoulder ached and his neck throbbed as he readjusted Zoe. Nearing exhaustion, Jonah pushed through an unlocked door to his left and set her down. Going back to close the door he scanned the small room. Lightning attacked the sky outside providing him just enough light every few seconds to look around.

Unknowingly, Jonah had stumbled into a chemistry lab. For the laymen, this meant nothing; but for a man with his training, this was a gold mine. Jonah ran from shelf to shelf inspecting the items. In between strikes of lightning he fixed his eyes on the dim hallway outside the glass on the door. The hallway was motionless and silent. Jonah found the first chemical he was looking for. *Jackpot.*

Snatching a rag from the shelf, he poured a little ammonia into the center and, returning to Zoe, hovered it right below her nose. Groggily, she roused, laying her head back against the corner of the wall. Jonah applied a little more and brought it back up to her face. This time she coughed a little and looked up at him.

"Jonah?" she asked weakly.

"I'm here, Zoe. How do you feel?"

"Tired. They put me in a room… on a bed…there was a doctor…"

"It's okay now. I'm going to grab some things, and then we have to move again. I need you to do your best to wake up, okay?"

****

Sitting against the wall, Zoe did her best to listen. She could hear drawers opening and bottles rattling. Occasionally, during the red lightning strikes, she could see his silhouette against the grey walls. The lightning flashed; he had moved again. Another flash, another location. Zoe played *Where's Waldo* with her twice now savior until she felt strong enough to climb to her feet. Her arm burned where they had injected her and her stomach churned. Afraid to scratch her arm, Zoe stumbled through the darkness in search of Jonah, but a few steps later, vertigo seized her. Searching for, and finally gripping a table, she tried to clear her head.

Coming out of the darkness with a flash of red lightning at his back, Jonah grabbed her other arm and helped her towards the door.

"Are you able to walk?" Jonah asked softly.

"I think so; I'm dizzy."

"They gave you something; but we're going to get out of here. I've got a friend in the other camp. He can help you."

She nodded, trusting him completely. "What are you carrying?" she asked, noticing a bucket full of bottles illuminated by another flash of red lightning.

"Everything we need to make a bomb," Jonah replied.

CHAPTER 49

Clark couldn't be certain how long they had been in the tunnels, but he knew he was starving. The feeling of his grumbling stomach sent new fears through his body. *How could they possibly escape?* The world above was completely irradiated. They couldn't possibly hope to get out. *Would there be a rescue effort? Could the nation muster one in time to prevent them from dying of starvation first?*

After some thought, Clark decided he needed to move down the tunnels on his own and make it west into the Fairfax metro station in Virginia. He had taken the train many times. He knew where he was: at the Orange line station on Potomac Avenue. He knew what he had to do: walk on the same line until he reached the end of the rail. Clark estimated it was about 20 miles, a long walk, but how could he just wait? He had to get out, and he had to do it now.

As Clark stood up to leave, the boy that had clung to him for the past few hours stood up as well. "Where are we going?" he asked.

"We?" Clark retorted with a snort. "I'm taking a walk; you need to wait here for your family." Clark knew there was no family to wait for, but he couldn't have this kid tagging along.

"Are you getting food?" The boy asked, seemingly ignoring Clark's previous comment. "I'm starving."

"There's no food." Clark insisted. "I have a long way to walk…" he paused. Looking around, he knew there was no way the boy would survive without someone to help him. For whatever reason, despite his disdain for children, Clark felt sorry for the boy. "Never mind," Clark told him. "Let's go get food," he said, reaching out his hand. "What's your name anyway?"

"Bobby," the boy said excitedly. "I'm six," he bragged, "and I could eat a whole rhinoceros right now!"

"I'm 25," Clark retorted. "Maybe we could find a rhino to eat at the zoo?"

Bobby laughed and Clark smiled. Hand in hand, he led the youngster through the dark; delicately stepping over the sleeping stranded that seemed to number in the thousands. Clark knew if they didn't get out of the Metro soon, it would get ugly down here. Very ugly.

CHAPTER 50

On the move again, Jonah propped Zoe up with one arm as he carried the bucket full of chemicals in the other. While she was still a bit woozy, he was grateful she was able to move on her own accord and the farther they walked, the more capable she became. In his frenzy to find chemicals, he came across a few gems which were now contained in the five gallon painter's bucket. He had a butane lighter, one small propane tank, an oxygen tank, bleach, ammonia, and a roll of duct tape. He also found 12 inches of five inch wide PVC pipe. While he had hoped to find some ammonium nitrate, he wasn't surprised when he didn't. What he had would have to make do.

Jonah chose to continue down the hallway to the left from the door, and then take the first right. As they continued to move, one thing became certain to him; they had left the hotel and were now in some sort of underground laboratory. Had the lights been on, he may have noticed the transition from hotel to lab and was slightly disturbed that he had missed that detail. Regardless, the long carpeted hallway had given way to slick linoleum tiled floors. The walls were no longer wallpapered with cartoons of rocket ships and planets, either. Instead, they were replaced with long windows that enabled scientists to look in and observe experiments.

Jonah was even further disturbed to find the labs were not only in pristine shape, but they looked used; and recently. A lab coat was draped over a chair, a beaker of blue fluid sat on a scale, and a centrifuge spun a red substance Jonah believed could only be blood. This was not what he expected to see in a colony allegedly on the verge of collapse, in a colony ravaged by war, or one whose inhabitants were, in the words of Jillian Jaspers, "desperate to leave." No, as they walked past the labs, Jonah became certain this was not just an unused space that was forgotten after the war. This was a place that was being used and it was being used frequently. The question was, for what purpose?

The hallway narrowed and curved towards the right. After some distance the enclosed hallway ended, revealing one final room on his left. Compared to the darkened hallway, the room itself was brightly lit. As Jonah approached the large room, black letters etched in a bright silver plaque on the side of the door explained its purpose: "Examination Room #4."

Halting in front of the room and peering through the large window, Jonah could almost feel the horror that had occupied the room only a short time ago. In the center, there was a single bed with a large light hanging above it. Although it had been scrubbed clean, blood streaked the floor as if the wounded had drug her body to a wall to rest her burdened soul. Scratches from bloodied fingernails marked the walls, and a tuft of long hair lay in the far corner of the small ten by ten room - suggesting its occupant had pulled out her hair in a final act of desperation.

"Is this where they bring people to die?" Zoe asked, clearly perceiving what Jonah was also observing.

Jonah pulled her close to his side and attempted to obstruct her view. "Ignore it, Zoe," he tried to order, but could hear the meekness in his own voice. After Zoe's ordeal, he found himself once again terrified that he had not gotten to her in time, but suddenly realized in the rush to escape, he had forgotten to look her over.

"Zoe, did they give you anything?"

Zoe looked up at him, her face was coated with fear. Beads of sweat had formed along her forehead as she surely came to the same realization that Jonah had. Raising her arm she revealed to Jonah a small pinprick along her vein on the inside of her elbow.

"Is that all they gave you? That shot there in the arm?"

Zoe shook her head no. "They said that was for the pain. They put a big needle in my side." Lifting her shirt, Jonah could see bruising and a much bigger puncture mark on her left side just below her last set of ribs. "It hurt like hell," she told him earnestly.

Jonah kept his arm on her shoulder and pulled her back, close to his chest. While he felt terrible, there was nothing to do but continue moving. He didn't know where Jillian and her group of miners were searching, but they would certainly come down these lab hallways sooner or later, and Jonah didn't want to be here when they did. Zoe was strong, but in under a week she had arrived on an unfamiliar planet, watched her parent's murder, and was now subject to a sadistic experiment only God knew what. Sooner or later, Zoe would break; and Jonah needed to get her to a safe place before she did.

Jonah turned with Zoe still in his grip down the hallway. Instead of ending, the cinderblock lined wall that should have signified the end of the road was cracked and torn away. Stones were piled up on either side of the opening and dust from the excavation had been sloppily swept into piles. Through the opening, Jonah could see the familiar red rock of subterranean Mars. This was exactly what he was looking for; a way out! The earthquake Jillian described earlier must have opened up this far wall – but why it was further cleared out, he couldn't be certain.

They walked down the hallway together, arm in arm, towards the entrance of the caverns. Peering through the opening, the musty dampness erupting from the belly of Mars blasted him in the face. But there was another smell. A smell like soil. In fact, it was so rich, Jonah's mind was flooded with memories of a rainy spring day in Maine. Leaves that were once concealed by the winter snow and exposed by the warmth of the sun's rays became home to earthworms, centipedes, and the like. The longer he thought about the rotting leaves, Jonah found himself acutely aware of yet another smell. Before he could put his finger on it, Zoe called it out.

"Yuck. It smells like rotting eggs!" Zoe exclaimed, scrunching her nose and moving her free hand back and forth in front of her face.

CHAPTER 51

Zoe clung close to Jonah as they descended the carved staircase into the caverns of Mars. She tightly wrapped one hand around his large forearm and held the other close to her stomach. With each step her side ached, and soon it didn't just ache, it burned. Zoe had never been one to become lost in imagination, but the recent events had her head spinning. *Just what had they injected into her? What would it do?* As she pondered, the aching became worse, and soon it felt as if a hangman's noose had been tied around her insides and was being twisted tighter and tighter.

Jonah continued walking, appearing not to notice Zoe's distress. And maybe she didn't look so bad, but she felt it. Maybe they didn't inject her full of anything; maybe they just took something from her, and then she wouldn't die. Another shot of pain rippled through her insides and shoved optimism into a corner of her mind. She started to sweat more heavily and felt light headed.

"Stop tugging me along." Zoe complained at last. "I've got to sit down." Her breathing picked up and soon she felt as if she was going to hyperventilate.

Jonah examined her face. He looked worried. "Let's get you down these stairs and we can find a place to sit down," he said, gently, faking a smile.

The smile didn't help, but she was glad he took her seriously. "I don't think I can make it. This really, really hurts." And, it did. In the short time they had stood still, the pain from her stomach ripped upwards and outwards towards her skin. The pressure against her ribcage was so intense she thought she might explode. Zoe keeled over and grabbed her stomach with both hands, letting out a labored grunt causing Jonah to drop the chemical bucket to try and steady her with both hands.

"There's a landing just ahead," he said. The pain was so intense, Zoe could see his lips moving but couldn't comprehend what he was saying, and soon felt herself being carried down the rest of the way. The sensation that had once been restricted to her stomach now flowed through her veins. Her veins burned as if her blood itself had become molten lava, too thick to flow easily through her constricted blood vessels.

Zoe let out an agonized scream as Jonah rushed her to the platform to get her into a position that was more comfortable. She could never understand why she would hear some people beg for death when they underwent intense suffering. Now, in this dark cavern, without her mother or father, Zoe caught herself praying for death. She no longer feared it. It would be her release.

****

The child's shrieks echoed down the hallway and found Jillian's party from behind. The group spun around in unison and faced down the darkened hallway leading to the labs. None moved however. Every miner in the group knew what was fabled to be down that hallway. They had heard screams down these hallways on many other nights while guarding the darkened corridors below.

Finally, an exasperated Jillian Jaspers goaded them onward. "Let's go!" she shouted. "He's getting away with our girl!" Looking blankly at each other and then at her, the two men in the front finally started moving down the tunnel towards the labs.

The party of eight, seven of whom carried clubs, walked quickly down the hallway towards the labs, towards the screams, and toward an area they dared not go to on their own. It was an area where the rumored horrors were the makings of nightmares. It was the lair of the grootslang.

Jillian pumped her arms ferociously trying to keep up with the longer-legged security guards she had managed to rally in the wake of the girl's rescue. Jonah didn't understand what was at stake. His "rescue" of the girl could ruin everything. But she didn't necessarily blame him. After all, she had never told him what was at stake. Why Zoe was so important to their cause.

And what was at stake exactly? Creating a new earth on Mars? Terra-forming the planet to sustain permanent life? No. It was bigger than that. Much bigger. Out of breath, Jillian felt herself getting angrier as she considered just what was on the line. *This wasn't about some colony. This was about the future of the human race! Couldn't he see that?*

The party slowed as they walked past the labs. In an effort to ensure he was not hiding in one of the rooms, three men broke off to the left to clear the Blood Room, as she called it. Jillian had stopped referring to it by its actual name for some time. To give her miners direction she simply referred to each laboratory by its primary purpose. The one they stood in front of now was used to analyze blood; specifically, the effects of certain biological agents on blood and a person's immune system. She recalled how many hours they had spent locked away, performing experiments on rodents, and monkeys, and worms. Not many animals survived; but the ones that did, those are the ones whose blood now sat in vials, locked away in the cabinets waiting to be reexamined.

The men exited the Blood Room and moved down the hallway a little further to a room on the left. The Chemical Room. Technically, it was laboratory number three and its real function was the storage and mixing of chemicals. It contained centrifuges to mix blood with unique chemicals, dye specimens, and sterilize instruments. Only one animal had lasted long enough to make it to this room. It was the least of creatures, but the most important to their mission here.

"Do you hear that?" one of the men asked Jillian, interrupting her chain of thought.

"No, what?" She responded, leaning her head to listen down the hallway intently.

"Nothing. That's my point Jillian. The screaming has stopped." The other three came out of the room and all of them looked to her for guidance. Jillian was tired of making obvious decisions.

"What are you staring at me for?!" She exclaimed louder than she had planned. Reducing her voice to a stern whisper she continued. "If she's dead we still need her body to examine why it didn't take. If she's not dead, he's moved her farther away. Keep going!"

With a heavy sigh, but compliant nonetheless, the guards turned and moved briskly down the hallway, continuing their search of the rooms.

****

The sound of voices alarmed Jonah more than ever. Jillian and her gang must have been close; too close, and they were certain to have heard Zoe's screams. Jonah looked up the stairwell to where he left his bucket of chemicals and back down at Zoe. He had propped her up against the rock wall on the small platform postured above a large cavern. With one hand on her shoulder and his other placed on her neck, Jonah felt for a pulse. Her heart still beat and he could see her chest rise and fall with each breath.

Jonah looked up at the stairwell again. He didn't have much time to mix the chemicals before the party would be on them. Just as Jonah prepared to make a dash to the bucket, Zoe woke. Her eyes were hazy and Jonah could tell she struggled to figure out what had happened.

"Zoe," Jonah whispered, with his hands on her shoulders. "How do you feel?"

"I feel okay," she responded groggily. "How long was I out?"

"Just a few minutes. Zoe, I need to get to that bucket of chemicals. Are you okay by yourself for just a moment?"

Zoe's eyes had shifted past Jonah and appeared to go out of focus. She was looking something behind him. "Is that blood?" she asked.

Jonah turned around to see dried blood covering most of the platform. He hadn't noticed it when he carried Zoe down the stairs, a realization that shocked him. *What was going on with him? When did he throw twenty years of training out the window?* There was so much dried blood that it looked like an artist had poured it onto the ground and dashed more across the wall; perfecting a yet-to-be-seen masterpiece. As if someone had spilled a five gallon bucket of dark red paint and was planning to coat the entire cavern with it. Jonah wanted to investigate but the sound of voices and the scuffing of feet brought his attention back to the immediate danger. Jillian.

****

"And you are certain you checked every corner? Every stinking nook and cranny?" She fiercely asked one of the miners.

"He's not behind us," the man responded definitively; then, seeing the suspicion across her face he added "he went down there," pointing through the hole in the wall that led to the caverns.

Jillian surveyed the group that was with her. They looked scared. Despite her attempts to keep their experiments secret, the whole colony had circulated rumors about the events in the labs and deep below the Martian surface. While she was certain they didn't know much, they knew enough. And they didn't just look scared, they *were* scared. But it wasn't just them, Jillian was scared, too. What they had created… that worm. It wasn't controllable. In their attempts at terraforming the planet for life, they had experimented with a few too many genes… a few too many combinations. But this would reconcile all of that. They were so close, so close and all they needed to do was find the girl. Examine her if she was dead to see where they went wrong. But if she lived. If she lived! That would be ground breaking. Calming herself, Jillian surveyed her group.

"We're right behind them. Get down those stairs and either find them or find a body!"

****

Jonah dug into the crimson soil furiously with his hands and thrust the PVC pipe into the ground as hard as he could. "Pack around this with dirt," he ordered Zoe, pointing at the foot long PVC pipe. As Zoe packed, Jonah lit the small butane lighter and dropped it inside the pipe. This would serve as his mortar tube and initiator. He could see light from flashlights, now wrapping around the stairs, from their pursuers. Jonah looked at Zoe. "Faster," he whispered aggressively. "Pack it tighter. It has to be tight, Zoe!" he whispered again.

Pulling the duct tape out of the bucket, Jonah stacked the two tanks end on end so that the oxygen tank was on top. Next, he taped them wildly together and went in search of a rock. Jonah could see the first group's feet descending down the stairs. Soon they would be on them. Racing back to Zoe with his homemade mortar and newly found rock, Jonah pushed her out of the way just in time for the first two to appear fully down the stairs. The two saw him and stopped on the stairs just as Jonah struck the end of the propane cylinder with his rock. Nothing. A second time. A third. Finally, after the fourth strike he heard the familiar hiss of propane firing out of the tank.

"Bomb!" the miner shouted as Jonah dropped the improvised mortar into the tube and threw himself over Zoe to protect her from the blast. The two tanks erupted from the PVC pipe just as Jonah had hoped and exploded into the wall just in front of the retreating miners. The impact of the oxygen tank against the rock wall caused it to rupture, catching fire from the heat of the burning propane and exploding as a result of overpressure in the tank itself. In a massive burst it sent shrapnel up the stairs and slamming into the retreating miners.

Jonah heard the miners erupt in howls of pain. He rolled off Zoe, grabbing his bucket in one hand and her arm in the other and lifted them both off the ground. "Get down the rest of the stairs!" Jonah ordered her. She opened her mouth to speak, but his ears rung so badly he couldn't hear a word she said. Regardless, Jonah assumed she got the message because she turned and left the platform for the cavern below.

Looking up at the explosion, he could see trickles of fire simmering along the steps that led up to the lab. As Jonah's hearing returned, he could tell there was coughing and wailing from above. The bomb had worked perfectly, and now it was time to complete their escape.

Jonah twisted the top off the half gallon bottle of ammonia and added it to the bucket. Next he took the bleach and, as he removed the cap, a familiar voice called to him from the top of the stairs. It was Jillian.

"Damn it, Jonah!" She shouted. "Damn you. Damn you!" Jonah didn't say a word. He just waited. Her voice didn't get any louder to indicate she was coming any nearer, nor could he hear her feet scraping down the stairwell. She finally spoke again. "Just tell me if she's alive. Did she make it or is she dead like the others?"

Jonah looked down at Zoe. She was alive. *But he hadn't thought that was the end of it. Could that have been it? Would she be okay?* He looked back to the stairwell and made the decision to speak. It would give away his position. It would let her know where he was. But maybe she wasn't going to pursue them any longer. "What if she's dead?" Jonah shouted back, listening to his echo bounce off the walls and up the flight of stairs.

"It doesn't matter Jonah. If she's dead she's dead. You won't stop us. More girls will die to perfect this." She paused. "But if she's alive Jonah. If she's alive, we've uncovered all the mysteries we need to survive on Mars. If she's alive, all the other deaths would not be in vain."

Jonah kept his eyes locked on the stairs. "How long did it take them to die?" he asked.

"Hours, Jonah. Just hours… does that mean she's alive?" She asked expectantly; excitedly.

Jonah wasn't sure how to answer. *Did they not need her? Was Zoe just a test subject of whatever formula they had invented? Did they already have what they wanted but just had to verify its host?* Jonah looked back down at Zoe. She had heard the same statement and hope was forming on her face as well. Jonah picked the bleach back up from the hardened platform and for the first time noticed his hands were bleeding from digging into the rocky soil a few moments earlier. Pouring the bleach into the bucket Jonah looked back towards the stairwell. The fire still simmered but no shadows descended the passageway. "Don't follow us!" he shouted back as a pale green mist began to rise from his concoction.

CHAPTER 52

Logan Carter raced in his four-door pickup truck along I-70 just east of Indianapolis. The mid afternoon sun shone brightly in his rear view mirror, and, from the looks of the crowded city streets in Indianapolis where he had detoured for fast food and gas, the Midwest was faring far better than the east and west coasts. Despite the bustle of the city, however, there was the weight of the awful truth that several million people had just been obliterated from the face of the planet. The mood in Indianapolis was somber, but whispers erupted all around him as he entered the McDonalds to use the bathroom and place his order. Rumors flew and Logan listened intently as he stood in line to pick up any tidbits that might help him on his journey.

"I heard from a trucker that DC was completely destroyed," proclaimed an older gentlemen to his friend.

"An invasion? But who?" whispered another woman, cutting her eyes to the window, perhaps expecting a row of Russian tanks to suddenly appear at the drive-thru.

Back in his truck, Logan pressed hard on his accelerator and swerved into the left the lane to pass a smaller car. His desire to reach Virginia was driven by fact, uncertainty, and fear. The facts, as he knew them, were so terrifying and inflammatory that the only way he could possibly share his knowledge of the truth was in person. His uncertainty was driven as a result of the events from the last twelve hours and his inability to make contact with anyone in charge. For hours, Logan had waited for somebody to rescue him from his bunker while searching desperately for a cell phone or radio signal he could use to communicate with someone. All of it was useless. It was as if the entire nation had blacked out, and to Logan, that meant there was something more than a nuclear bomb detonation.

After trying to reach authorities, he knew what he had to do. He had to tell someone who it was that raided the bunker. His attackers spoke Mandarin to each other; therefore, the Chinese were unmistakably behind the attack. Now, twelve hours into his drive, racing at speeds of nearly 100 miles per hour, he was only seven hours from his destination. His head throbbed, his jaw ached, and his heart pounded, but he felt greater purpose in this moment than at any other in his life. While there was no announcement on television, Logan knew he would find a delegation of politicians in a nuclear missile bunker south of Roanoke, Virginia. If any had survived the initial blast, this would be the location of decision-makers, and what he needed were decision-makers.

Logan hastily unwrapped a Big Mac from its package and spilled ketchup lathered lettuce all over his already filthy blue jeans. Not bothering to look down, he shoved the burger into his mouth and accidently jerked the steering wheel; nearly losing control of his truck. *All in a day's work when trying to save the world*, Logan thought to himself. After almost being disintegrated into atomic particles by a nuclear warhead, Logan had sworn he was going to get into better shape. Twelve hours into his drive, however, he decided he would save the diet for a time after he saved the world.

Logan shoved another bite into his mouth and checked his cell phone. Still no signal. He accelerated faster, swerving back into the right lane. *Just wait until they hear what I have to say*, Logan thought to himself. He desperately hoped he'd get to Virginia before the delegation decided to attack the wrong country!

Suddenly, Doubt jumped into the conversation and spoiled his heroic dreams. *Why would anyone believe a fat nuclear tech actually knew who attacked the bunker?*

Logan pondered Doubt's question while he sipped on his Diet Coke, washing down a full pickle slice. Feeling it slide slowly down the back of his throat, he answered Doubt with full conviction. *Because I learned Mandarin in college and studied in China for six months!*

Studied in China? Learned Mandarin? Sole survivor of the blast? You'll be arrested! Viewed as a traitor, a collaborator! Doubt answered him.

"No!" Shouted Logan out loud, accidently spitting some coke back up from his throat and bouncing the pickle slice off the back of his tongue, restarting its slow decent back towards his belly. *They'll have to believe me,* he responded to Doubt once more. *Why would a traitor drive over a thousand miles to warn them that the Chinese were attacking? I'll be hailed and remembered just as Paul Revere was!*

You would drive there to kill the survivors though… if you were a traitor.

Logan didn't have a response this time. He couldn't respond. In part, he realized that Doubt was right. Doubt was almost always right, fear and uncertainly never formed out of nothing. It seized hold of the tiniest speck of a concern and magnified it. But there was another reason Logan couldn't respond. The pickle he had swallowed, which was actually attached to a half chewed up piece of bread had stopped sliding and became lodged in his throat. He coughed violently, but to no avail.

At over 100 miles per hour, the spasms of a choking man could wreak havoc on a poorly maintained pickup truck, and soon, Logan found himself headed for a ditch. Swerving to stay on the road, his tire buckled and then exploded. Sparks erupted from the wheel as metal made contact with asphalt and at the second jerk of the steering wheel to correct his fishtailing vehicle, the truck went into a full roll, bouncing from side to side, disintegrating the steel cab around Logan as he rolled. Sliding on its top, the white Chevrolet Silverado was eventually halted by a light pole. Upside down and suspended by his seatbelt, Logan let out only one more cough. As his vision faded he could feel a trickle of blood run down the side of his face to form a drop on his ear. Logan was no hero and certainly no Paul Revere. His warning would die with him; thwarted by the poorly chewed pickle from his favorite hamburger.

CHAPTER 53

Charlie had been through a lot during his career, but nothing could prepare him for the situation in which he now found himself. After climbing off the Boeing 747, busses transported them about an hour west, into a location called Granite Ridge. Technically speaking, Granite Ridge didn't exist, at least, not until today. The site had presumably been chosen because of its remote and defensive location deep in the Blue Ridge Mountains.

Upon arrival, Charlie sent his executive officer to find the chief of security, while he and his subordinates walked the perimeter fence, speaking with secret service agents and integrating soldiers into their existing security perimeter. His first concern would be security, but that meant a lot of research. Charlie had to determine roads that led up to the facility and plan weapon systems against those. He sent scouts to look for foot traffic, deer stands, animal trails, and water sources. If this place was going to house the surviving members of the United States government, it needed to be entirely locked down.

After Charlie walked the perimeter, inspected the food and water sources, and issued orders to the men under him, he went to find his executive officer. The facility itself was huge and looked like it was an old mining shaft that had been converted into a cold war missile bunker. The perimeter consisted of concertina wire atop a twelve foot chain link fence around the outside of the facility. The fence created a half moon around the mountain and anchored into the rock on either side of the shaft's opening. Red lights lit the entrance and an electronic key pad combination opened the heavy concrete door leading to the shaft itself.

Following a thirty second elevator ride, which Charlie estimated was a three hundred foot drop in elevation, the elevator opened up to an expanse of concrete reinforced walls, hallways, and office space. Florescent lights lined the ceilings. Just beyond the entryway, he could see his executive officer speaking with a secret service agent.

"Hey Todd, what've we got?" Charlie interrupted, walking up to them. Todd was in his mid-twenties. His jet black hair, athletic build, and thick jaw complemented his intelligence and drive. Most importantly, Charlie trusted him with his life.

"We're finalizing the security and sleeping arrangements, sir." Todd replied. "The secret service is stretched pretty thin. They have twelve guys total, primarily manning the gate and personal security around Mr. Wilkes. They work twelve hours on, twelve hours off, so really, we can only count on about six of them at any time." Todd repositioned to make sure that Charlie could see that the agents were only armed with hand guns, and quickly tilted his head to make sure that Charlie knew what to look at. "There are two fifty-person bays just down the hallway to the left, those are for us. The guest quarters and offices are a bit farther down. Mr. Wilkes and his team are in the command center at the end of the hallway. I set up our comms in there as well, but we don't have anything yet. All this rock is making it a bit difficult."

Charlie nodded, and patted Todd on the shoulder. "Keep up the good work. Let me know when we have our mortars up and the routes mapped out. I want two recon and surveillance teams patrolling nonstop. Get with top to figure out the rest and chow plan." With that, Charlie excused himself from the agent and walked down the hall to find Mr. Wilkes but hardly made it even a few steps before bumping into an old friend. "Evie, is that you?!" he shouted with delight. She was the best thing he had seen in a long time, and relief instantly flooded his insides like food nourishing a deprived body.

Evie, just as shocked as Charlie, let out a gasp, and then gave him a tight hug. "Charlie! I had no idea they were going to send you."

"It's great to see you again," Charlie said warmly, pulling out of the hug to grab her hands and look at her face. "I heard about what happened to Jonah. I'm truly sorry, Evie." Charlie paused to give her enough time for that comment to resonate and then changed the subject. "I was just headed to find Governor Wilkes. We're here to secure you guys."

"I'm glad it's you." She responded. "I'll take you to him. We have a lot to do before the Chinese envoy arrives.

CHAPTER 54

Donning her lab coat, Jillian Jaspers dove head on into her work. She didn't have the time to pursue Jonah any longer, and soon, nobody on that side of the camp would be of any concern. She suspected that if Jonah knew what the next days would hold, he wouldn't have bothered trying to save Zoe. The scientific breakthrough of the century was upon them, and she just needed a few more minutes to change history forever.

Jillian delicately inserted the 20 gauge hypodermic needle beyond a porous rubber barrier and into a yellowish green liquid. Even though she had only been working for a short time, her neck already ached from the tense and high stakes work of genetic manipulation. Jillian watched the liquid goo fill the clear compartment at the back of the needle.

Finished with the draw, Jillian removed the needle and rotated her chair to the left to overlook her life's work. Beyond the safety glass, was a greenhouse style room with three tables covered in a dark green and brown mossy substance. In the moss were hundreds of tiny, yellow, mucus sacks. The pale yellow ovals didn't measure more than an inch long, but inside them contained all the genetic information required to create thousands of the creatures she had come to call grootslangs – a mythological fanged snake of the underworld.

Zoe had proven her immune system to be resilient enough to cohabitate with the grootslang DNA. Now, in the small vial extracted from the rubber sack, Jillian had replicated Zoe's DNA and planned to insert it into her grootslang, forever uniting Zoe and the grootslang as an unbroken bond through shared blood.

While her creation was already capable of surviving on the subsurface of Mars, it hadn't been capable of reproducing. Zoe would help with that, but it wasn't just the grootslang that received all the benefits. Zoe was the first born of a new race. A race capable of surviving in the environment that the grootslang created. A race capable of living on far less oxygen and far more carbon dioxide. A race capable of living in far less atmosphere and far more radiation. Over the next several months, Zoe would transform into a perfect human being, capable of surviving in the harshest conditions, not just on Mars, but on hundreds of other planets as well. Soon, very soon, Zoe and the grootslangs would become one race, pushing forward with one purpose, the true colonization of Mars.

Jillian proudly inserted the vial into a tube that carried nutrients into the cocoons. Soon Zoe's blood would mix with the grootslang and they would become a symbiotic creature; the only creatures capable of cohabiting and flourishing in such an inhospitable place. She knew they would cohabitate because before Zoe, there was herself. The only other human, whose immune system would not reject her precious creature; the only other human who's DNA was forever mixed with the grootslang. Where Jillian could not volunteer to become the mother of a new race, however, Zoe had stepped in. Not voluntarily of course, but history wouldn't remember that; only the success.

Jillian typed and sent an email on her computer, printed and shoved a copy of her crowning achievement into her briefcase, and pushed away from her desk. She could see fluid pulsing through the tubes and being devoured by her babies below. Turning to leave, she took one last look at the lab and her creation inside it. Soon they would hatch and transform the very face of Mars, but in that transformation, anyone left behind would not survive. Jillian strode proudly out of the labs and back towards her room in the hotel. Soon, very soon, she would say goodbye to the red planet forever.

End of Book One

ACKNOWLEDGEMENTS

A huge thank you to Sarah Keller, Andrea Keller, Amber Axline, and Kristin Leeman for reading copy after copy and providing lots of feedback.

Thank you to all those who have read this book, especially those that have taken the time to review my work, I'm eternally grateful for your reviews and cherish the moments I get to interact with my readers.

ABOUT THE AUTHOR

Thane is a graduate of the Virginia Military Institute with a degree in psychology and a minor in English. Following college, Thane married his high school sweetheart Sarah, and started his career as a cavalryman in the United States Army. After over twelve years of service, he has deployed to both Iraq and Afghanistan where he was personally engaged in ground combat. His service has thus far earned him two Bronze Stars and numerous other awards and decorations.

Relying on his psychology background, military experience, and Christian faith, Thane writes novels that seek to explore human nature under dire circumstances, the reality of pain and suffering, and the resilience of individuals to accomplish super human feats. Thane's hopes are that as readers experience his character's journey through the gift of reading, readers will be greater equipped to endure the inevitable ups and downs in life itself and dream to accomplish greater things.

In addition to his wife Sarah, Thane is blessed to have four wonderful children that do all they can to keep him from pursuing his love of writing.

PREVIEW FRACTAL
SPACE

Available July, 2016

PROLOGUE

"I'm telling you, brother, our time has come," the young man whispered, barely able to keep his teeth from chattering.

Draped in the white fur of an animal native to the planet Coridon, the two men huddled together in a hastily built ice cave as the temperature outside plummeted to fifty below zero. They had trained with each other since they were children and were now prepared to graduate together as warriors. All that remained was one final test: survive a week on Mount Horeb. It was simple enough to just survive—the most basic of tasks. But considering that that task meant surviving on a floating mountain in the middle of the Northern Sea during winter, this test became an entirely different story.

"How can you be certain?" his best friend responded, turning his head to look over his shoulder. The two leaned back to back, supporting each other's weight as they shared a tiny white-haired rodent that they had captured in a snare the day before. It was hardly big enough to sustain a child, let alone two grown men, and as Brokk crunched down on the small bones, he knew that the meat wouldn't give him the energy he needed to survive the night.

The Jarks graduated their officers in an unorthodox fashion. While most systems believed that prior to graduation a culmination should be a demonstration of the things one had learned and how they are best applied to interstellar combat, the Jarks believed culmination should be focused inward—on oneself and the qualities that must be honed in order to lead great men into battle.

Brokk thought he agreed, although not entirely at this moment. Teachers had repeatedly drilled tactics into his head for years, and warfare had been the primary subject of debate around the table with his family as well as in class with his peers. He understood warfare, but he had never experienced it.

Surviving on Coridon gave him this opportunity, and in the days he had been there, Brokk had already learned more about himself and what it took to survive than ever before. There would be no help, and many of his brothers over this week would die. But those who survived, those who made it, they were the future, forged on the icy peak of the coldest habitable planet of the galaxy and ready to do battle on behalf of their people.

Brokk's teeth continued to chatter as he tried sucking the

marrow out of the rat's leg bone before throwing the very last fragment into his mouth. "Because you and I are going to graduate tomorrow," he managed to sputter out.

"We won't survive the night if we don't get any more food. I can't keep warm," Lago complained.

He was right. They had to go out again. In the face of utter exhaustion and frigid temperatures, calories were essential, and right now, calories were what the two of them lacked. Brokk pushed himself to his feet and offered a hand to his red-skinned friend. "Then let's hunt," he said with a grin, trying to show courage in the face of extreme doubt.

Flame from their candle danced and glistened off the icy walls of their hastily built shelter, and Lago's white teeth shone from behind long strands of gray fur draping off his hood as he returned an eager smile. "I'll lead," he said at last, accepting Brokk's hand and pulling himself to his feet. "Besides, I'm a better tracker than you anyway."

The fierce wind howled as they left their shelter in search of food. Merely stepping out into the cold sucked the breath from their lungs and left the two gasping for frigid air to fill their blood with the oxygen they so desperately craved. Brokk staggered into the snow, trying to catch his breath, and imagined that this must be how it felt to be sucked from a damaged hull into the lifeless void of interstellar space.

One following the other, the two aspiring warriors tilted their bodies away from the wind and attempted to walk perpendicular to it.

Facing into the freezing blast would send icy daggers through the openings in their hoods and could permanently damage any exposed skin on their faces in mere seconds. Silently, the two trudged through barren trees, using webbed snowshoes to keep them on the surface. With each step, pain shot through their bodies from lifting fatigued legs. Their arms, heavy and worn, strained as they painstakingly drove ice prods into the ground ahead to ensure that they weren't about to fall through a weak patch of snow and land in a gully. A prod to the left and a step with the left foot. A prod to the right and a step with the right foot. *Prod, crunch, prod, crunch, prod, crunch, prod.* It was slow going, and Brokk's stomach roared with hunger. Finally, Lago turned around to face Brokk.

"I'm lost!" he shouted over the wind. "Which way was the canyon?"

"I think you're right," Brokk responded, motioning forward. Lago shrugged and turned again to continue his movement. The wind wailed as the storm drove snow off nearby peaks and pushed bursts of icy sleet into their faces, but the two pressed onward, further away from their camp and into the coming night.

Lago continued to lead. *Prod, crunch, prod, crunch, prod, crunch, prod.* The rhythm captivated Brokk and took his mind far from icy blasts, painstaking steps, and frozen fingers. In his desperation for comfort and aware of its power, Brokk allowed himself to be mesmerized by it, focusing on nothing but the familiar noise. *Prod, crunch, prod, crunch, prod. Prod, crunch, prod, crunch.* Silence.

Lago was gone. "Lago!" Brokk shouted, running to the spot

he had last seen him. "Lago!" he bellowed again, fearful that the wind blew his voice back into his throat rather than outward toward his friend. Through the wind and snow, he approached a small ledge; Lago lay twenty feet below, unmoving. "Lago!" he shouted again from his hands and knees, careful not to lean too far over the small pit that had opened up from the weight of their steps.

Lago twitched his mitt-covered hand and groaned. "I think I broke my leg!" he finally shouted.

Brokk could see the snow beneath him turn a reddish hue as it absorbed blood from his now-exposed wound. *Broken…and maybe worse.* But beyond the blood-stained snow was a far more terrifying sight. On the other side of his narrow ridge, a dense nitrogen-composed fog began to climb up from the valley below. At a frigid minus 320 degrees, the gas would not simply freeze Lago; it would make him feel as if he were on fire while turning the blood in his veins into solid ice.

"I'm coming down there for you," Brokk bellowed back, grabbing at the climber's rope he had looped over his shoulder and searching for a nearby anchor point.

"We'll both die," Lago shouted back. "Don't!"

It was too late. Brokk was a man of action and had already secured the rope to a tree and tossed the remainder down to the gorge below. Rappelling to the bottom, he rushed to disconnect his rope and deploy the emergency avalanche shelter he kept in his backpack. The gas had reached the ridge now, and icy fingers stretched out from the fog, begging Brokk to let it feast on their exposed skin. Finally at Lago's side, Brokk gripped his shoulders and pulled him into the small pup tent, which was barley large enough for one man. "I guess we'll both die then," he muttered into Lago's ear, zipping the tent behind them.

CHAPTER ONE

Brokk stared intently at the red-streaked sky as beads of sweat rolled off of his golden skin. The eight-foot tall, broad-shouldered behemoth was large, even for Jarkian standards, but he was a half-breed, and mixes between Tassis and Jarks were known to be some of the most formidable warriors in the galaxy. In part, this is why the Jarks were able to live a relatively peaceful existence—there were few people who cared to challenge them and even fewer who lived to brag about a victory against the massive creatures.

Unfortunately, there was another reason the Jarks remained largely unchallenged in their corner of the galaxy. All the planets in their solar system were oversized and orbited either too close or too far from their star. While two of their planets remained in the habitable zone, they just barely did so. The Jark home world, and the one that Brokk currently resided on, was a wretchedly hot planet with an immensely dense core. Its sheer size exerted such gravity on the creatures that were unfortunate enough to live on this planet that their appearances were significantly different compared to more fortunate life elsewhere in the galaxy.

Their second planet, Coridon, rested just within the habitable zone on the other side. While Jark rarely dropped below one hundred and twenty degrees Fahrenheit, Coridon was a winter wonderland that never rose above thirty degrees Fahrenheit. The two twin planets, enormous in size and barely habitable, had masked the Jarkian existence for millennia and allowed them to develop into the race they were today with minimal interference. When the Jarks finally did announce themselves to the other races throughout the galaxy, a galactic order had been established and few cared to break galactic law and challenge the new race.

This peace, however, didn't prevent the Jarks themselves from seeking something greater. For centuries, Brokk and his forefathers had been taught about a great injustice that was dealt their ancestors by the hands of the Tassi. They knew there was a solar system that was rightfully theirs, a solar system that they had been cheated from, and one that would make life easy for all Jarks if they could get it back. Even though Brokk had never seen a picture of Tassi, he felt it calling to him. Returning to Tassi was his destiny.

Brokk stared intently at the sky because tonight, this very night, he was to command a legion of starships to attack the Tassi system. He had studied for years and understood Tassi tactics. Scouts had already been dispatched and reported the size and location of Tassian defenses, and Jark artillery was prepared to fire interstellar munitions at his command. Most important of all, the loosely affiliated galactic order was too incompetent to halt their unannounced advance. By the end of the month, the Tassi system would belong to the Jarks and Brokk would become their chancellor.

Brokk was ripped from his reverie by his best friend, Lago. The two had grown up together, fought together, and were now reaching for the prized system together. There was only one final matter to attend to: a sacrifice to the dead in exchange for a blessing on their campaign. This was a tradition that dated back far beyond Brokk's ancestors, and a tradition that he would certainly not forsake.

"Dreaming about Tassi?" Lago shouted with a smile from behind. Lago was pure Jark and was significantly stouter than the golden-skinned half-breed. Lago's skin was a reddish bronze and was covered in a swirl of curly dark hair. He stooped slightly, preferring to rest his thick arms on the ground to support his large torso. While the Jarks often walked upright, the thick atmosphere and weighty gravity caused them to develop a preference for resting on all fours.

Despite his caveman-like appearance, Lago was a brilliant mind who was devoted to the study of applying astrophysics toward military tactics. The two of them were inseparable and, despite having no blood connection, were closer than brothers could ever hope to be. At Lago's approach, Brokk brightened, and any fear or doubt he had about the mission before them suddenly dissipated.

Brokk, whose Tassi genetics insisted that he remain standing upright, spun around to greet him. "Lago! I had hoped you'd come find me!" he responded, smiling and opening his arms for a warm greeting.

The two embraced each other and separated again. "I wouldn't miss it for the world. We've come here together every time before leaving home…you know how much I like the cliffs," Lago responded, shifting his gaze to the city beyond.

Brokk knew, and Brokk loved the cliffs himself. The massive rock structure jutted out over the volcanic rock below and provided a spectacular view of both the city and the sea, and no matter which way one turned, the ferocity of the world was captured in an unmistakable majesty. The outcropping's thickness allowed it to hang for hundreds of meters beyond the shore line—and the men always insisted on stepping out onto the farthest point.

"Did I ever tell you why I come here each time?" Brokk asked.

Lago, now standing upright and shoulder to shoulder with Brokk, shrugged, indicating that he had never thought about it. The star they orbited was a red giant, at the end of its stellar lifespan, and rays imbued with deep reds and oranges constantly bombarded the atmosphere of their massive home world. Red clouds, engorged with a mixture of water and sulfuric acid, stretched across the burned orange sky.

"This is why we'll win," Brokk answered, giving him a moment to reflect before continuing. "Look at this place. It's awful!" he joked. "There isn't anyone tougher than a Jark."

Lago laughed. "You have to remind yourself that?" he asked, still chuckling.

"It helps," Brokk responded with a grin. Brokk turned his shoulders and pointed toward the sky to show Lago what he was looking at before he had arrived. Just off the nose of the cliffs to the north, a massive battleship could be seen maneuvering along the skyline. The ship's bronze, dual-pronged nose was unmistakable against its dark gray exterior. It was Brokk's, and it was the head of the armada conducting its final checks before joining the remainder of the fleet in the upper atmosphere. "Are you ready, Brokk?" Lago asked.

Brokk stared at Lago for a moment longer before returning his golden eyes to the horizon. "I've never been more ready in my life, Lago," he insisted. "We're a battle-hardened fleet, and with you by my side, we are unstoppable. The promised system will be ours again." Brokk looked down at his red-and-black battle uniform. Red was reserved for ship and fleet commanders and helped the crew tell them apart in the heat of a battle. On his wrist was a holographic display that could project information anywhere. In battle, he often allowed it to hover data in the corner of his eyes so that he could see everything at once; during planning sessions the device depicted three-dimensional displays to help his commanders visualize the battlefield. Today, he simply used it to tell the time.

"The artillery bombardment should be commencing soon. We'll

start getting updates within the hour," Lago responded.

Brokk smiled. Jark artillery was second to none in the known universe. They had developed a weapon that was capable of firing explosives from outside a planetary system by creating temporary shortcuts through space. The Jarks would chose a planet not more than a few light years from their target, establish an artillery platform, and then create temporary wormholes with which to sling rounds onto the planet below. The system was stealthy and dreadfully effective. Best of all, it was nearly immune to a counterattack. An entire planet's computer systems and defenses would be consumed by locating and defeating the source of the barrage while the armada attacked from the opposite side.

"I'm going to reward you when I become Chancellor," Brokk said. "You'll live better than you ever have."

Lago didn't respond and the two turned to walk back down the rock face toward the offering below. An infant Jark lay helpless, naked, and screaming on a black stone platform. The hardened volcanic stone rocked gently as it floated in a soupy mercury pool that bled from the planet's interior. Brokk's watch flickered and vibrated on his wrist, indicating that it was time to ask the gods to bless his cause. On cue, six Jark priests, robed in gold, stirred the mercury bath beneath the child. As they stirred, they hummed in monotonous unison.

The words they sang were unknown to all but the six who sung them. This was the language of the dead, and as they stirred the mercury it began to boil, reflecting the deep red streaks from the sky above. The silver soup bubbled and popped, the baby rocked violently back and forth, and the priests suddenly erupted in loud chanting, inviting their dead—the souls of billions—to accept this innocent sacrifice and give them the military victory they required.

Hands now appeared—filthy, hair-covered hands, coated in the slime of the mercury and taking on the colors of the sky above. Brokk counted one at first, but like the heads of a hydra, the hands slithered and grabbed at the rock, desperate for the crying infant bathed in the warmth of the life that he possessed. Suddenly, the rock flipped, the hands disappeared, and the humming stopped. Their ritual was over. The dead had accepted Brokk's sacrifice; he would achieve the victory he desired.

Silently, the six priests and two commanders descended from their rocks to their city below. "I think I'll miss this city," Lago finally said.

"We'll build an even greater one on Tassi," Brokk boasted.

www.ingramcontent.com/pod-product-compliance
Lightning Source LLC
Chambersburg PA
CBHW061024120726
47910CB00006B/2090